THE GUN LORDS OF
STIRRUP BASIN

Texas Ranger Luke Kimlock started against the town. He wanted to drive out the two men that had gunned down Kimlock's uncle in the process of raiding Stirrup City. Kimlock and his newly found brother, Wobbly Head, try to take back what is theirs while finding everyone on the take. In a land where the law is only a piece of paper, the two have to take it into their own hands to rid the town of the gun-hawks before the outlaws get rid of the town!

LEE FLOREN

THE GUN LORDS OF STIRRUP BASIN

Complete and Unabridged

LINFORD
Leicester

A-1

First Linford Edition
published April 1989

Copyright © 1977 by Manor Books, Inc.
All rights reserved

British Library CIP Data

Floren, Lee, *1910–*
    The gun lords of Stirrup Basin.—Large print ed.—
Linford western library
I. Title
813′.52[F]

ISBN 0-7089-6680-2

Published by
F. A. Thorpe (Publishing) Ltd.
Anstey, Leicestershire
Set by Rowland Phototypesetting Ltd.
Bury St. Edmunds, Suffolk
Printed and bound in Great Britain by
T. J. Press (Padstow) Ltd., Padstow, Cornwall

1

FORTY-FIVE in hand, tall Luke Kimlock worked his way silently through the high buckbrush to come in unnoticed behind the ambusher. "Turn aroun', Concho!" he said harshly.

Luke's savage words brought the heavy-set bushwhacker hurriedly to his boots. Winchester rising, the man whirled to stare at Luke, surprise scrawled across his dark face.

"Don't raise that rifle," Luke Kimlock warned. The ambusher stared at Luke's naked .45. Eyes narrowed dangerously, he then looked up at Luke. "Who t'hell are you?"

"I'm the man you aimed to shoot out of saddle as he came ridin' down yonder trail," Luke Kimlock said.

The man laughed harshly. "I wasn't havin' my rifle over this boulder to shoot at anybody ridin' down off the rimrock. I was still-huntin' a buck deer that hangs out in these diggin's."

Luke Kimlock slowly shook his head. "I

heard you an' Neefy talkin' about half-an-hour ago, Concho."

"Neefy?"

"Yes, when you rode out to relieve him."

"You're—You're Luke Kimlock?"

Kimlock said, "I am. I spent the night up in the sand boulders on the rimrock over us. My horse was tired and I had a hunch there'd be trouble waitin' me if I rode down that trail."

Concho's wide tongue wet his thick lips. Montana's new day lit the high cheekbones of his wide face. Concho's piggish eyes were riveted on Luke Kimlock's rigid .45 Colt.

That gun pointed directly at Concho's heart.

"I saw you leave Stirrup City," Kimlock said, "an' head this direction. I couldn't figure out why anybody would ride out that early so I kept my field-glasses on you."

"An' you heard me an' Neefy talkin'?"

"I did. Sound carries good in this high altitude."

"Why would I want to kill you, a stranger?"

Kimlock said, "I got my uncle's letter two weeks ago in Cheyenne. He said his life was in danger. He asked me to ride north. And here I am, Concho."

Concho said, "An' what's next, Kimlock?"

"I'm takin' you into Stirrup City. I'm turnin' you over to the law there. I'm filin' the charge of attempted murder against you."

Concho's surly laugh showed blocky, tobacco-stained teeth. "Kimlock, I kin see you ain't never bin in Stirrup City. That town has no law—that is, no lawman. Two men run it an' this basin."

"An' you work for them?"

"That I do."

"So then there's no use my takin' you into town? These two would just set you loose?"

"You learn fast," Concho sneered.

Luke Kimlock said, matter-of-factly, "Then I might just as well kill you here and now, Concho?"

Concho hurriedly said, "Oh, I'll go with you, Kimlock. You got me under your sights, man. I'd be foolish to raise this rifle an'—"

Luke Kimlock deliberately baited the killer. His .45 lowered slightly. Concho had his rifle's hammer eared back, Kimlock had noticed. Eyes dangerous slits, thick lips open, Concho fell for the ruse.

His Winchester started up. It moved with liquid rapidity. Concho knew how to handle the

3

rifle. The barrel leveled, pointing at Luke Kimlock's heart. The hammer fell.

The rifle snarled.

Concho was fast—but not fast enough. He took Luke Kimlock's lead flatly in his barrel-like chest. The bullet dropped him to his knees. His rifle fell, its bullet plowing uselessly across space.

Boots spread wide, .45 smoking, Luke Kimlock watched the ambusher, no emotion on his twenty-four year old face. He had no sympathy for an ambusher. To him, ambush was the lowest on the scale.

Had he not shot Concho, Concho would have shot him. It was that simple, that elemental.

Concho never shot again. Neither did Luke Kimlock. No other shots were needed.

Head down, Concho raised both hands, clamped them against his chest, where blood immediately covered them.

Slowly, methodically, Luke Kimlock reloaded his .45, face set, stony, eyes on Concho.

Concho's mouth dropped open. Then Concho fell forward on his belly, arms flung out, rifle lying smoking just beyond reach. Concho never moved again.

Luke Kimlock pulled air deep into his lungs. Then, gun again on hip, he climbed the rimrock where his buckskin awaited on picket, the horse hidden by the high sandstone boulders.

Standing there on the rimrock lip, outlined against the scarlet morning sky, he looked down into Stirrup Basin, the magnificent unlimited sea of grass and rolling hills stirring his blood.

Stirrup River meandered across the wilderness of grass, brush and trees. Small side creeks ran into the river. Eight years gone his uncle, Cyrus Blunt, had trailed Texas longhorns into this area.

Cy was his dead mother's only brother. According to Cy's letters, which had been yearly events, the transplanted Texan had established his ranch headquarters five miles up river from Stirrup City.

Kimlock had never before seen Stirrup Basin. Always his lawman duties had taken him to this wild town, then that. He'd been in Cheyenne when his uncle's letter had arrived addressed to Ranger Luke Kimlock, Wyoming Rangers, Headquarters, Cheyenne, Territory of Wyoming.

Within twenty-four hours, Luke Kimlock had headed north, buckskin seeking a mile eating trail lope. And now here he stood on Stirrup Basin's southern rim, a man he'd killed lying limp and bloody in a clearing below, the rough shale of the downward trail leading eventually to Stirrup City.

Dang ol' Cyrus, anyway! Hadn't mentioned what kind of trouble faced him. Just asked that his nephew—the one he'd reared from babyhood—ride north right off and help him.

Kimlock had immediately noticed that the letter's stamps had been cancelled not in Stirrup City but in Beaverton, although the letter had asked him to come to Stirrup City.

A map of Montana Territory had shown Beaverton to be some forty miles east of Stirrup City. Why hadn't his uncle mailed the letter from Stirrup City?

Twenty minutes later, leading Concho's horse, the dead ambusher tied belly-down across his saddle, Kimlock rode down from the rough country and headed for Stirrup City, the early morning sun already gaining heat.

The heavy buckbrush petered out as he came to the gentle foothills.

That was good. Grass had more fattening value when brown, Luke Kimlock knew. Sage-

6

brush and greasewood grew along with the grass.

Kimlock noticed that where greasewood grew there was less grass. He remembered his uncle's spread down in Texas' Big Bend country, where he'd been reared by Uncle Cy, for his mother had died when he'd been only two years old, his father having been killed by a bronc before his son's birth.

Greasewood grew there also, but there the Texans called it chamiso—and where chamiso grew the soil contained alkali and alkali soil supported less grass than where sagebrush grew, for sagebrush would not grow in alkali.

But this was wonderful cow country. High grass and water and timber along Stirrup River and the creeks running into it to provide summer shade and winter windbreak, not to mention a continuous supply of good water.

Cattle were in good shape, spring calves trotting beside fat cows. Luke Kimlock saw freshly burned brands on the calves' right ribs. Quarter Circle V, the iron.

What brand did Uncle Cy burn? Kimlock didn't know. If it were Quarter Circle V, Uncle Cy ran good blooded cattle stock.

Kimlock saw saddle-horses, too. They were

not in as good shape as the cattle. He figured calf-roundup had just ended. The saddlers had been ridden on long, tough circles.

The cattle were spooky. They saw him and ran away, calves kicking and jumping. Apparently they wanted nothing to do with a rider.

The broncs also were wild. They threw up tails upon seeing him, snorted, faced him, pawed the earth—then ran away. Kimlock never got close enough to read the brands on the saddlers.

Luke Kimlock liked the looks of Stirrup Basin. It was almost as good a cow country as Texas' Big Bend, although winters in the Big Bend mountains would not be as tough or as long as winters here on this high northern range.

Uncle Cy had picked good cow country.

He came upon a wagon road one mile from Stirrup City. The road was dusty and very deeply rutted.

Kimlock studied the ruts. To make imprints that deep the road had to be traveled by wagons hauling very heavy loads.

He turned in leather. He followed the ruts east with his eye and noticed for the first time a low, flat cloud hanging in the still air against the faraway hills.

He judged the dust to be at least miles away. Vision was almost unlimited in this pure, clear air. Did a moving herd of cattle raise that dust?

He knew cattle and cattle raising. It was far too early in the summer for beef roundup. Cattle didn't raise that dust.

Then what did—?

He straightened in leather. That faraway eastern dust cloud was no concern of his. He followed the wagon-trail west. When he rounded the toe of a long hill, Stirrup City lay a mile ahead.

A lone freight wagon came his direction, two span of lumbering oxen pulling the high wheeled Conestoga. An old skinner walked beside the high front wheel, oxen prod in hand.

Luke saw the handles of fresnos and slips and other dirt moving equipment sticking up over the wagon's high sides. The graybeard halted his oxen.

"That a dead man you got across that saddle, cowboy?"

Luke Kimlock nodded.

The old man went forward. He buried a gnarled hand in Concho's dark hair. He lifted the ugly, blood face. He looked at it for some time. His face had little emotion.

Finally he let the head drop. "Gunny by the name of Concho, cowboy. Been aroun' Stirrup City for nigh onto a year, now. You kill him off?"

Luke Kimlock nodded. "Ambush."

"The world lost nothin'. I don't spend much time in Stirrup City. Jes' pass through on my way to Hangton, up in the mountains west. Railroad runs in there. I freight outa there."

Luke nodded.

The oldster seemed to want to talk. Luke Kimlock knew freighters lived lonely lives and when they met you they could talk your ears off.

"Hangton's almost a hundred miles due west in the Little Rockies. Got this equipment in there years ago when the bigwigs opened up an open fill copper mine but gold paid the best so they went underground an' I freight this stuff to the railroad camp where they need it to move dirt buildin' the right-of-way."

"Railroad?"

"Yeah. You kin see the dust cloud way off to the east. Goin' run rails through Stirrup City

10

—that is, if the bigwigs get the right-of-way permits lined up."

Luke Kimlock thought, that explains that faraway dust cloud. He brought the subject back to the dead man.

He learned that Concho—and Neefy—worked for Deacon Stebbins and Silver Brennan. Brennan owned and operated a saloon in Stirrup City. Deacon Stebbins owned the only bank.

"They're partners in the Circle Diamon' cattle-ranch," the oldster said. "Deacon's a cripple. Dunno what happened to him. Stays upstairs in his bank all the time. Fiddles a lot, 'specially when things go wrong."

"Fiddlin' banker, huh?"

"Mighty tough man, though. A year ago had some trouble with a Texan ridin' through. Texan got the best of Deacon's cashier for a hundred bucks or so."

Luke Kimlock nodded, listening.

"Some mistake cashin' a check, er sumpin. Texan wouldn't give the DINERO back. Deacon sent a gunnie against him. Texan took the pistol away from the Deacon man an' pistol-whupped him silly."

"Then what happened?"

"Somehow, Deacon got down them stairs, they tell me. Called the Texan's hand, an' Deacon with his gun in leather. Texan made his play. I never seed it, but they said the Texan was a fast one."

"Who won?"

"Deacon shot him through the heart, just like that—afore the fast gun could let his hammer fall. By the way, what's your name, cowboy?"

Luke Kimlock told him. "You know Cy Blunt?"

"Only by sight. He runs Quarter Circle V cattle. Brands big right ribs. What about him?"

"He's my uncle."

"Uncle, huh?" The oldster spat tobacco juice over a grasshopper on a sagebrush stem. "Had a mite of tough luck, I understand."

"In what way?"

"He was ambushed!"

Luke Kimlock studied the seamed, weather beaten old face. His voice seemed to come from a distance. "How many days ago?"

"Well, lemme see. This Wednesday, all day. I went through Stirrup City four days back. He'd been ambushed day afore that, if memory's right. That'd make it Friday, wouldn't it?"

"Who ambushed him?"

"I dunno. I jus' heard the talk when I went through Stirrup City, that's all. None of my business so I—

"Where was he buried?"

The faded gray eyes studied Luke Kimlock, a sudden twinkle sneaking into their depths. "I guess I got ahead of my story, young man."

"In what way?"

"You're uncle was ambushed, yes—but he ain't dead."

Relief flooded Luke Kimlock.

2

TWENTY minutes later, Luke Kimlock rode down Stirrup City's mainstreet, the dead man still jack-knifed over saddle, behind. And, as he rode, Luke Kimlock took the layout of this pioneer town into his memory, all three blocks of it.

He'd seen dozens of similar towns, ranging from the Mexican-Texas border to this high northern area, just forty or so miles south of the Canadian Line. All clung much to the same pattern.

Although the hour was early, already some were astir on Stirrup City's boot hammered thick plank sidewalks. Kimlock glanced leisurely at these men, cataloging them as cowhands, an occasional prospector and a few dirt men, evidently in town from the railroad camp.

They watched him, stared at the dead man, said nothing. When Luke Kimlock was opposite the Town House the gunman Neefy came outside and halted on the edge of the

14

planks, his eyes small and pulled in his thin face, his thumbs hooked in his gunbelt ahead of his holstered .45.

"Ride over here," Neefy ordered.

Luke Kimlock grinned, tense inside. He neckreined his buckskin to the right, halting the animal in front of Neefy, who studied Concho lying across the bloody saddle.

Without Neefy noticing, Luke Kimlock loosened his right boot from stirrup.

"That's Concho," Neefy said.

"That's Concho," Kimlock assured.

Neefy raised hard eyes. "Who killed him?"

"I did."

"An' who the hell are you?"

"Luke Kimlock, Neefy."

Neefy scowled. "How'd you know my name?"

"Heard Concho call you Neefy when he rode out this mornin' to spell you off where you an' him had the ambush spot that you hoped to kill me from," Kimlock said.

"You were camped up on the rimrock?"

"I was."

Neefy said, "Thought I heard a mite of noise up there when I was on guard last night. Aroun' midnight, huh?"

15

"Later. About two, my Ingersoll said."

Neefy nodded. He and Luke Kimlock might have been discussing the time of the day, nothing more. Onlookers, though, were coming, attracted by the dead man.

Neefy's right shoulder moved slightly. Luke Kimlock said, "You pull your gun, Neefy, and I'll kill you."

"You sling a fast gun, Kimlock?"

Luke Kimlock shrugged. "I'm still alive. A few of the others aren't. That prove anything?"

"Might and might not, Kimlock. You're ol' Cy Blunt's nephew, I take it."

"I am. An' he's been ambushed, they tell me. You laid in wait to shoot me in the back. Maybe you shot down my uncle, too?"

"An accusation, Kimlock?"

"You can take it as you want, Neefy."

Neefy nodded. "I'll think it over." He turned without another word, and Luke Kimlock restored his right boot to stirrup, watching Neefy enter a saloon that bore the title: STIRRUP CITY SALOON, Silver Brenna, Prop.

Kimlock was ready to turn his buckskin to ride toward the town livery barn at the street's end when he heard the violin playing.

16

The music came from the second story of the two-story brick bank on the near corner. Kimlock read another legend: Stirrup City National Bank, D. E. Stebbins, Banker.

The second story had two big windows. One was open, white curtain moving slightly to the warm breeze. And, through it, he saw the violinist.

The man stood by the window, bow moving rapidly. Luke Kimlock could see him clearly.

Deacon Stebbins' face was long and wedge-shaped with pinched, thin lips. He was of medium height. A blue suit-coat covered stooped shoulders. He wore a white shirt and black bow tie.

The violin was tucked under the scraggly chin. Despite distance, Luke Kimlock saw small, beady eyes. Those eyes were on him. They were sharp and probing and the bow rose, fell, the music one moment angry, the next peaceful and serene.

Luke Kimlock stored the wizen face in his memory and rode toward the livery, the sound of the violin following him, then stopping as he rode into the barn through the high arched doorway.

The interior was dark. Horses stood in stalls.

Luke Kimlock caught the good smell of horse-flesh, saddle-blankets, saddles and gear. A stoop shouldered oldster, plainly the hostler, shuffled out of the small cubicle set in the far corner.

Luke Kimlock swung down. "Grain my buckskin an' go heavy on the blue joint," he said and then, jabbing a thumb at Concho and Concho's horse, "Whatever happens to them two is the business of whoever Concho worked for."

"Did you—kill him?"

"I certainly did," Luke Kimlock said. "An' don't ask me where an' why, because I'm gettin' tired of answerin' same. They say he drew wages from a saloon man named Silver Brennan an' a banker named Deacon Stebbins."

"Them two own most of Stirrup City. An' they control most of the rest."

Kimlock unloosened the front cinch of his double-rigged kack. "They don't own much if they own this burg."

"They come here about two years ago."

Kimlock unloosened the backaberry buckle on the back cinch. "Where'd they come from?"

"Nobody seems to know."

Kimlock threw the rig over the saddle-pony. He went to the buckskin's head and removed

18

the bridle, slipping it down under the hacka-more BOSAL "They tell me the banker's a cripple."

"Got that way right after comin' here."

Kimlock hung the bridle over the saddle-horn. He began unbuckling his Cheyenne legged leather chaps. "Come all of a sudden over him?"

"Right like that. Doc Miller don't know yet what hit Stebbins."

Kimlock laid his chaps over his saddle-seat. He unbuckled his star-rowled Garcia spurs. "He play the violin then?"

"Yeah. Some say he used to play big concerts somewhere back east or somewhere like that."

Kimlock hung his spurs over a nail driven into the stall post. "Anybody come to search my stuff tell them to save their time, cowboy, 'cause they ain't a damn thing in my bedroll that'd interest anybody. Only one thing might draw their attention. That's a letter from my uncle."

"Might I ask who's your uncle?"

"Cy Blunt."

The hostler gasped. Kimlock adjusted his holster by shrugging his thin hips. He bowlegged out of the barn, the sound of the violin stronger now—judging by its stern, chopping tones Deacon Stebbins really was riled.

He met a middle-aged heavy-set man going toward the barn. "I'm Doc Miller. I'm also town undertaker. They sent me after Concho's body."

"Who's the they?"

"I'm not at liberty to tell, Mr. Kimlock."

Luke Kimlock nodded. "I'll find out sooner or later. I judge they to be Stebbins an' Brennan. Have you treated my uncle?"

"No."

Kimlock frowned. "Another doctor in this town?"

"No, I'm the only one."

"I don't understand."

"I work on salary for Mr. Brennan and Mr. Stebbins. My contract with them doesn't permit me to treat anybody else without their permission."

Luke Kimlock said, "Doesn't that go against your professional oath?"

Doc Miller laughed. "The Hippocratic Oath? That's where the word HYPOCRITE comes from, isn't it?"

The medico entered the barn. Luke Kimlock headed for the Steerhorn Cafe, across from

Deacon Stebbins' bank. The violin had stopped. He was glad of that. The see-sawing had been getting on his nerves.

His uncle had written that the Blunt ranch was five miles up Stirrup Basin River. He'd eat and then head out after his buckskin had been grained and watered and rubbed down by the old hostler.

He glanced toward Silver Brennan's saloon as he entered the cafe. A muscular, thick-set man stood beside the swinging, batwing doors. The man watched him.

Kimlock entered the cafe. He took a stool near the front window. A young woman asked, "Your order, sir?"

"A stack of wheatcakes, please. And plenty of coffee, black."

"Coming up, sir."

The girl went to the back of the cafe and repeated the order through the window to the cook. Luke Kimlock looked about. He was the only customer at the counter on a stool.

A man and woman—elderly people—occupied a booth. They were the restaurant's only other customers.

Luke Kimlock looked back at the saloon. The heavy-set man was approaching the cafe.

21

The girl had returned. Kimlock murmured, "Silver Brennan?"

"Silver Brennan," the girl said.

Brennan entered. He said good morning to the waitress and added, "A cup of java, please," and slid his bottom onto the stool at Kimlock's left.

"You're Luke Kimlock."

"Are you askin' or statin'?" Kimlock asked.

"Could be both."

Kimlock looked at the man. Brennan had the earmarks of a hard case, no two ways about that. Brennan was of average height but very broad and the muscles of his thick shoulders bulged his silk shirt and set off his big head in a bold and ugly dominance.

His face was full and square, corpulent and heavily-jowled and his faded blue eyes, set small and tight in that beefy face were shrewd and sharp with the bright hotness of animal intelligence.

"What do you want, Brennan?" Kimlock asked.

"Why'd you kill my hired hand, Concho?"

Kimlock said, "You must be jokin'?" The waitress slid his hotcakes in front of him, his cup of steaming coffee following. "If you came

22

in here to ask foolish questions, Brennan, I think you've made your point."

Brennan's jowls reddened. "You got a wise-acre tongue."

"And a fast gun," Kimlock coldly said. "You send another ambusher against me an' I kill him, too. An' then, you know what?"

"What?"

"Then I'll kill you for sendin' him against me." Luke Kimlock glanced up at the waitress. She'd been close enough to hear his statement. For the first time, he paid her masculine attention.

Jet black hair peeped from under her white linen cap. And Kimlock saw, in that one glance, that she possessed a dark, savage beauty, her eyes black pools of womanhood.

Her sweet face showed fear. She was moving slowly down to the long counter's far end, eyes on him and Brennan. Luke Kimlock looked back on Stirrup City's gun boss.

Silver Brennan studied his coffee cup. "There are some things I guess you should know, Kimlock. Me an' Deacon Stebbins now own your uncles Quarter Circle V ranch."

"How did you get it?"

"We bought it on a tax deed. Seems as

though your uncle forgot to pay his property tax an' the county filed foreclosure and Mr. Stebbins and me bought the ranch."

"Try another joke," Luke Kimlock said.

Brennan looked at him. His eyes were narrowed now and savage. "Elaborate, please, Mr. Kimlock?"

"First thing, my uncle always paid his bills, far before the time they came due."

"He's had money troubles," Brennan pointed out. "He claims cow thieves are rustlin' his Quarter Circle V cattle. When he trailed to market last fall, somebody hit his beef herd a dark night. He lost over a thousan' head to thieves, he said."

Luke Kimlock nodded. "Who could these thieves be, Brennan?"

"What'd you mean by that?"

Luke Kimlock got to his feet, wheatcakes and coffee finished. "I've not been here long, Brennan, but I've learned a few things. My uncle brands Quarter Circle V on the right ribs, huh?"

Brennan nodded, eyes sharp on Kimlock.

"You an' this Stebbins animal run a brand also on the right ribs, but your iron is Circle Diamond. That right?"

24

"Right, but what are you drivin' at, Kimlock?"

"Simply this, Brennan. You make the quarter-circle into a full circle. You put another v—an inverted v—over my uncle's v. And what do you get? The v turns into a diamond."

Brennan said, "That's right, Kimlock. Then you're accusin' me—an' Deacon Stebbins—for runnin' a hot iron over your uncle's brand, an' changin' it to ours?"

Brennan also stood, now.

Luke Kimlock said, "It could be done, Brennan."

Silver Brennan's jowls turned blood red. He lost his grip and grabbed Luke Kimlock by the left shoulder, beefy hand twisting Kimlock's chambray shirt.

"Damn you, Kimlock! You came here lookin' for trouble an' by hell—?"

Kimlock cut in with, "Take your hand off my person, Brennan." His voice was low and cold with danger.

For one long moment, all hung in abeyance. Kimlock was aware of three outside points at once. First, there was the stolid Greek cook, standing in the kitchen doorway, bony and immobile, a cleaver in his right hand, his piggish eyes speculative and dangerous.

Kimlock wondered whose side would the cleaver be on? He looked at the elderly couple in the booth. The man had his gun drawn, letting the big weapon lie idly on the table.

Who would that gun fire at?

The dark-haired waitress had both hands under the counter. Luke Kimlock guessed she held a rifle—or a shotgun—

Who would she fire at?

Then, Brennan hit.

3

BRENNAN'S plan was simple.

He'd pull Luke Kimlock in close. Brennan was a saloon brawler, a rough-and-tumble man. He'd gouged eyes, use elbows, kick, bite—anything to win. Luke Kimlock had met Brennan's type before.

Kimlock lunged into Brennan. Brennan flung a curving right but it landed on Kimlock's back, a mauling gesture that had already spent its power. Kimlock hit with his left.

Kimlock also missed, but he used his elbow, cutting and smashing Brennan's bottom lip, bringing salty blood to the saloon man's tongue. Brennan staggered back, flashing out a left hook.

Luke Kimlock moved inside and the hook missed. He saw an opening. His right fist smashed it. His knuckles crashed flush on Brennan's blocky jaw.

Brennan changed his tactics. His right hand went down, clawing wildly for his holstered .45. This left his face completely defenseless.

Kimlock's next crashing blow drove Brennan against the far wall.

Brennan had his gun drawn. Another blow sent him reeling, gun slipping from his grip. It was a solid, deadly overhand right. Brennan crashed backwards. The door was closed. It had a glass panel. Brennan went backwards through the glass.

"You'll pay for that!" the Greek screamed.

The glass broke with the sharpness of a rifle report. Brennan went through to land on his back on the plank sidewalk outside. His .45 lay on the cafe's floor.

Luke Kimlock did not open the door. He merely stepped outside through the glassless panel. Brennan lunged forward from a sitting position, intending to entrap Luke Kimlock's boots and throw him.

Kimlock leaped to his right. Brennan's arms encircled thin air. Brennan's jaw was exposed. Kimlock coldly, convincing, kicked Brennan's jaw. Brennan went down on his face.

He didn't move. He was knocked out.

"Behind, Kimlock!"

The words came from the little waitress. She stood in the glass free opening.

Kimlock whirled, hand going down to his

holstered weapon. Two gunmen approached from the saloon. Already they'd sunk into the gunfighter's crouch—bent low, hands on guns, eyes watchful, faces deadly and stoic.

One gunman was Neefy.

A tall, angular man ranged on Neefy's right. Kimlock had never seen him before. His .45 rode well forward on his right thigh, his fingers taloned over its black grip.

His holster was thonged down. He walked ten feet apart from Neefy. They came slowly on, eyes on Luke Kimlock, who also had sunk into a gunfighter's pose, tall and ugly and deadly, eyes missing nothing.

Without looking back, Luke Kimlock said, "Miss, it'd please me mightily if you'd move out of the door. I don't want you to stop a bullet."

"Nobody's behin' you," a deep male voice said.

Luke Kimlock recognized the Greek cook's voice. It came from inside the cafe and to the far right. Kimlock did not take his eyes off Neefy and the gunman, but he reckoned the cook and waitress stood in the far corner, watching through the edge of the big plate glass window.

Stirrup City watched from a safe distance and safe angle. When Neefy and the gundog were thirty feet away Luke Kimlock said, "That's far enough. Another step toward me and I pull!"

Both gundogs halted, boots anchored in Montana dust. Luke Kimlock walked forward, talking as he advanced. He said, "It looks like I'll have to kill you, Neefy."

"I kin take care of myself."

"I doubt that." Kimlock looked at the other.

"I like to know a man's name before I send him dead to the dust," he said quietly. "What's your name, bucko?"

"O'Rourke. Tim O'Rourke."

"You work for Brennan an' Stebbins, I take it. Sling a gun for them, huh?"

"I do." O'Rourke wet his bottom lip. "I wanna ask you a question or two, Kimlock."

"Shoot."

"You was first with the Texas Rangers, when you was jus' a kid. Then you last carried a star down in Wyomin' Territory, right?"

"You're right, O'Rourke."

"You lawed durin' the Johnson County War some six months back, the way I heard it. The only Wyomin' Ranger assigned to that section."

"You're right again, O'Rourke. What're you drivin' at?"

"You busted up that trouble single-handed when you killed Kid Peterson in Worland, in a gunfight?"

"I did."

O'Rourke looked at Brennan, who still was out. He turned his eyes on Neefy.

"You can have him all by yourself, Neefy. I don't crave no part of Luke Kimlock. I seen Kid Peterson in action down in Arizony. He was livin' light with his cutter. The man who killed him—fair an' square—must be a real heller with a sixter."

Neefy said, "You white featherin' out?"

O'Rourke summoned a weak smile. "I'm too young to die, Neefy."

"They's two of us," Neefy pointed out, "an' only one of him."

"They could be six of us," O'Rourke said, "an' only one of him, but the HIM is Luke Kimlock. Mr. Kimlock, I'm glad you give me that information. I don't wanna commit suicide. I bid you goodday."

O'Rourke wheeled sharply, hand carefully held the proper distance from his gun. He stalked to a hitchrack. He untied a strawberry roan gelding, swung into leather, and turned the bronc to the north, loping past the bank.

He never got to the corner.

The rifle spoke from the bank's second story. Its bullet hit O'Rourke in the side of the head. The rifle spoke only once. Once was enough.

O'Rourke fell from his terrified horse. He sprawled in the street. He never moved. The horse ran on, reins dragging. It skidded around the far corner and out of Luke Kimlock's vision.

The rifle pulled back and disappeared.

Luke Kimlock took his eyes back to Neefy, who had turned very pale. "Good lord," the gundog breathed. "Deacon Stebbins killed him in cold blood. One bullet, no more."

"Maybe he isn't dead," Kimlock said.

Doc Miller knelt over the fallen O'Rourke. Apparently he overheard Luke Kimlock's words.

Doc Miller got to his feet. He brushed dust from his knees. "He'll never be any deader," he said.

Kimlock spoke to Neefy. "Why not get wise, Neefy? Why not take O'Rourke's way out—only don't leave town when Deacon Stebbins can see you?"

Neefy rolled that in his slow brain, seeking some way to use it. Now that he stood alone fear ran in his blood, pounded dully at his brain, and he wanted a way out.

This was not Neefy's way. Neefy's way was a bullet from the brush. Then Neefy saw his out.

"I never come to gun with you, Kimlock. I come to help Brennan to his boots."

Neefy lied, and Kimlock knew it. But Luke Kimlock, standing there on that dusty Montana street, accepted the lie, and let it pass.

"All right," Kimlock said.

Silver Brennan was coming to. He groaned, chewed his tongue, made gestures to rise. Carefully keeping his hand from his holstered gun, Neefy stepped by Luke Kimlock and, stooping, he helped Brennan to his boots.

Neefy worked Brennan's right arm around his shoulder and held him bodily, with Silver Brennan still bleary-eyed and groggy. Neefy looked at the waitress, who now stood in the cafe doorway.

Luke Kimlock then realized the girl had picked up Brennan's pistol.

Neefy said, "His gun, Miss Mary?"

The waitress' dark eyes looked inquiringly at

Luke Kimlock, who nodded and the girl handed the .45, but first, to Neefy, who turned and, using Brennan's big body as a shield, faced Luke Kimlock, Brennan's gun jutting.

Kimlock's .45 covered Brennan and Neefy. "Don't do what you're thinkin' about doin', Neefy," Luke Kimlock warned.

The waitress said, "I unloaded his gun, Mr. Neefy."

Neefy's eyes became dead. He said, "Damn woman," and poked the pistol, sight down, under his belt. Then, half-carrying the stumbling Silver Brennan, Neefy went across the street where the pair entered Brennan's saloon.

Kimlock said, "Thanks miss," and then, suddenly turning, he stabbed a glance at a window above the bank. The sun shone brightly into the window. He saw Deacon Stebbins clearly.

Stebbins did not now play his violin. He stood on crutches beside the window, his fingers long claws as he clutched the heavy drape. His eyes were on Luke Kimlock below.

Kimlock grinned satanically. He deliberately snaked up his gun, pointing it at the window. Despite his crutches, Stebbins quickly disappeared. Kimlock did not shoot. He'd had no intention of shooting. He'd just wanted to put the fear of death into the banker.

Kimlock holstered his weapon, looking up and down the dust. Doc Miller walked away beside two men carrying the limp O'Rourke between them. Kimlock then looked at the waitress.

"You're a brave woman," he said.

She smiled, then. Her teeth were white and even and she was very, very pretty in a self-reliant way. Her face held character, too.

"I was glad to step in," she said.

Kimlock grinned. "Because of me, a stranger?"

"Maybe," she said, "and maybe not. I'm Mary Burnett."

"You know my name," Kimlock said. "Seems as though all of Stirrup Basin knew I was ridin' in, an' I don't see how come. Unless my Uncle Cy spread word aroun', an' that ain't like him. He always was awful close-mouthed, especially in a tight."

"I don't know about that," the girl said, "but I do know that my father, Mack Burnett, used to run a small outfit out on Turkey Creek, a few miles east of here, where Turkey enters Stirrup."

Kimlock nodded, eyes on the bank window.

"A year ago night-riders hit our spread. Killed my dad—who was alone—and burned down our buildings."

"Silver Brennan?" Luke Kimlock asked. "An' Deacon Stebbins' gun-riders?"

"That pair own our spread now." Mary Burnett's voice was bitter. "They've done nothing but rob and kill since coming here from wherever the things came two years ago."

"How'd they get the land?"

"Through the crooked county officials in Beaverton. They work in cahoots with the crooks there. They claim your uncle's big ranch by the same vile procedure."

Kimlock nodded. "You did well when you unloaded Brennan's gun."

The girl laughed shakily. "I didn't unload it. I just said I did. And that ignorant Neefy believed me."

Kimlock still watched the bank's upper windows. He remembered the rifle speaking, O'Rourke falling from leather. This range had no law but what a man packed in his fists, in his holster—or his saddle-boot where his Winchester rested.

He was taking no chances.

"Come inside, Kimlock," the girl said, "and I'll put a little iodine on that small cut over your right eye."

The Greek had moved in behind Mary Burnett. Luke Kimlock saw he still carried his cleaver.

"You do no such thing, Mary," the Greek said shortly. "I want no trouble with Brennan an' Stebbins. I know who butters my bread, even if you don't."

He spoke in a heavy accent.

Mary Burnett said, "You think it wrong to help another human?"

The Greek shrugged fat shoulders. "Not when the human is hired by Brennan an' Stebbins."

Mary walked angrily back into the kitchen. The shiny sharp cleaver dangling, the Greek asked, "You pay for my glass in the door, gunman?"

Luke Kimlock shook his head.

"Why you not pay?"

"I didn't break it. Silver Brennan broke it."

"But you hit him. Your hit drove him through the glass, gunman."

"My name is Kimlock, not gunman," Luke Kimlock pointed out.

37

"To me you are just a gunslinger, a worthless killer."

Luke Kimlock had heard enough. There was no percentage in arguing with this Brennan-Stebbins man. "I'm not paying," he repeated.

The cook's face was red with rage. He raised the cleaver as though to throw it. He made an error. He paid no attention to Luke Kimlock's drawn .45.

The .45 spoke once, kicking back against Kimlock's palm. Lead ricocheted off steel. The cleaver went flying back into the cafe.

The Greek stared at his numbed hand. Finally he stuttered, "You shot it—out from my hand—An' you never shot my hand—"

Kimlock said, "Next time I put the bullet in your big gut, Alexander the Great."

Gun smoking, he turned, looked up at the bank's windows. One curtain moved slightly. He smiled mirthlessly.

Once again Deacon Stebbins had pulled back.

Grinning, Luke Kimlock entered the cafe, pushing the Greek aside. He went to the kitchen where Mary Burnett sat on a stool, face angry and disturbed. "You were goin' to doctor me, remember?"

She got to her feet. "You're a good shot. I

watched. That cleaver really went flying. I guess I'll fire that cook. He's getting so he thinks he owns this place."

Kimlock's brows rose. "He doesn't?"

"No, I own it. Lock, stock and barrel. He's worked for me about a year. Each day he gets more possessive."

Kimlock noticed the Greek stood in the doorway, with cleaver.

"You hear that, Alexander?" Kimlock spoke to the Greek.

"I heard," the Greek said. "I might go to cook for Mr. Brennan in his saloon."

"So long," Mary Burnett said.

The Greek began peeling spuds. Mary took a small bottle of iodine and some clean white clothes out of a cabinet drawer. "You've got blood on your forehead, Mr. Kimlock. It should be washed off, first."

"Where's the pump?"

"Behind in the alley."

They went out the back door, the girl carrying a bucket half filled with water. While Kimlock pumped, she poured water around the pump's cylinder to prime it.

Soon the plunger caught hold. Cold water cascaded into the bucket. Kneeling, Luke

Kimlock washed his face, water cold and sharp against his bruised skin. That done, he poured that water away, then pumped another bucket full.

He carried the filled bucket into the kitchen, where he set it on the sink. The girl then gently applied iodine to the small cut. When she had finished, Kimlock got to his feet.

"How much for the damages, Doctor Burnett?"

"Not a cent, Mr. Kimlock."

Kimlock said, "Doc Miller tol' me he treats only those who Stebbins an' Brennan says he can treat."

"That's right. They own him body and soul."

"And pocketbook," Kimlock added, looking at the glass-free front door. "Get somebody to put in that glass. I'll foot the bill, Miss Mary."

"Brennan broke it, not you."

Luke Kimlock looked at the Greek who evaded his eyes. "Alexander here said it right. If I hadn't hit Brennan he'd not gone through the window."

"Brennan will pay. He started the trouble. He grabbed your shirt. I'll see that he pays."

Mary Burnett's little jaw was set. Luke Kimlock got the impression that when the occasion demanded she could be strong willed and hard to get along with. He liked women with spunk.

He shrugged and left.

4

LUKE KIMLOCK did three things in Stirrup City. He went down the alley behind Deacon Stebbins' bank. A wooden stairway ran up from the alley to the second-story's door.

Across the alley was a wooden shed. A tough-looking customer sat under the shed's small wooden overhang. He balanced himself on the hind legs of his chair.

Luke Kimlock entered the alley, .45 in hand. The chair's front legs came hurriedly down. The man reached for the Winchester .30–30 leaning against the shed at his right.

Kimlock said, "Don't touch it, mister."

The grimy hand stopped. The man stared at Kimlock. "What'd you want?"

"Jus' passin' through," Kimlock said. "Jus' checkin' to see if the banker's got a guard guardin' his back door."

The guard said, "Well, you know, now. You're not climbin' that stairs, Kimlock."

"Odd how many Stirrup City people know

my name," Kimlock said, "an' here I jus' rode into town a while back, an' me a stranger."

"What'd you want?"

"Where's your post office?"

The guard stared through suspicious dark eyes. "What'd you want with the post office?"

"Might have a letter there. Mind tellin' me where it's located?"

"Not a bit, Kimlock. Right other side of Silver Brennan's saloon two doors, same side of Main Street."

"Thanks."

Kimlock walked backwards down the alley, .45 covering the guard who wisely made no move toward either his rifle or his sixgun. He was at the alley's far mouth when two men entered the strip a block away, hurrying toward Deacon Stebbins' stairway.

Kimlock flattened himself against the wall. Apparently neither man noticed him.

Silver Brennan climbed the stairs first, Neefy following him. The door on the upstair's landing opened. Brennan and Neefy disappeared inside. The door closed. But not before Luke Kimlock had a glimpse of Deacon Stebbins, balanced on crutches, violin in hand.

Luke Kimlock grinned, holstering his pistol.

Evidently Brennan and Stebbins were going to hold a council of war, with Neefy listening in.

He wished he could hear what would be said, but that of course was an impossibility.

Boot heels clomping worn planks, he strode toward the post office, Stirrup City's citizens discreetly watching. Across the street, Mary Burnett stood in her cafe's doorway, watching a man measuring the opening for a new pane of glass.

Kimlock crossed the street. "Brennan payin'?"

"Brennan is paying," the girl said.

Luke Kimlock continued on to the post office, keeping a careful eye on the windows over the bank. The postmaster was a burly individual of thirty odd, and he asked, "What'd you want?" in a rough tone.

"Information."

"Along what line?"

"I was slow in comin' up from Wyomin' because I had to tend to some lawman duties in Sheridan, but before I left Cheyenne over a week ago I sent a letter to my uncle Cy Blunt, at this post office. The letter should have arrived here about five days ago, to my reckonin'."

He grabbed the man's thick wrist.

"Leggo my wrist!"

Kimlock's grip tightened. "You opened that letter. Or else you gave it Brennan. Or to Stebbins. That letter told them I was comin' into Stirrup. That's how they knew to lay an ambush for me."

"I never gave nobody nothin'!"

"You lie, an' you know it. My uncle's letter came from Beaverton. He rode all that distance to mail it because he knew if he mailed it here you'd open it and read it an' let your two skunk-bosses know what it said."

"Kimlock, I'll—"

"You'll do nothin', mister." With his free hand, Kimlock moved an ink bottle close. He pulled his .45. Steel crashed down on glass. The bottle broke. Ink ran over the counter.

Kimlock holstered his gun. His hand left the struggling wrist. Both of his hands went behind the man's head. They pulled his head forward. Kimlock put on the downward pressure.

The man screamed. His mouth scooped up ink. Kimlock deliberately rubbed the man's face back and forth over the ink. Glass cut the postmaster's lips and nose.

Then, Kimlock pulled the head upward. He

twisted the head savagely. The man spewed ink as he yelled for help. Using the man's head as a purchase, Kimlock bodily pulled the man over the counter.

It was a feat of great strength. The man landed crashingly on the floor. Kimlock deliberately stepped on the postmaster's throat as he went out the door, sixgun in hand.

A crowd had gathered. They broke way for Kimlock who heard a woman say, "Thank God, a man—a real man—has finally ridden into Stirrup City."

The speaker was a middle-aged heavy busted matron. Kimlock touched his Tom Watson Stetson. "Thank you, madam."

"Rudd might come out with a rifle," the woman said.

Kimlock glanced back. The postmaster sat up, face smeared with ink, gasping for breath, both hands on his throat. "If he does, I'll kill him. Now can you tell me where I can buy some dynamite?"

"What're you going to do with dynamite?"

Kimlock kept a straight face. "I might blow up the whole town, madam. I'm in a vicious mood."

Beneath his joking front lay danger.

"Hardware store, about four doors south," the woman said. "Olaf Jenson runs it for Brennan and Stebbins."

"I thank you, madam." He holstered his six-shooter.

Olaf Jenson was a tall, bony middle-aged man. He stood in front of the hardware looking at the commotion in front of the post office. When he saw Luke Kimlock coming his way, he hurriedly beat a retreat into his store, locking the heavy oak door behind him.

Then, trembling, he peered out the corner of the big window, forgetting the sawed-off shotguns he had strategically located at various points within his establishment.

Luke Kimlock shook the locked door. It was of thick oak and had no give. He looked at Olaf Jenson beyond the glass. Then he lifted his gun from leather, the barrel came sharply down—and the big plate glass window's corner was rudely shattered.

Gun covering the shivering merchant, Luke Kimlock reached through the hole, turned the key in the lock, and opened the door and entered, closing the door behind him.

"Should be more considerate of customers,

Jenson," Luke Kimlock said, "and not lock the door in their faces."

"Silver Brennan will kill you!"

"I doubt that. He had Concho try this mornin'. Where's your dynamite hidden?"

"Ain't got none."

Kimlock said, "Look out the window, Olaf."

Jenson looked. The postmaster, face smeared with ink, was lurching upstreet, hands clutching his injured throat, some of the town kids following. The rest of the town—except for Brennan, Stebbins and their gunhands—apparently were out on the sidewalk looking on.

"Goin' to Doc Miller, I guess," the hardware man said.

"Either that or to report to Stebbins or Brennan. I guess I should have killed him."

"Killed who? Brennan?"

"No, I referred to the postmaster. But I guess I should have killed Brennan, too."

"He's tough."

"I didn't come here to talk about how tough a saloonkeeper is, Jenson. I came here for a half-dozen sticks of dynamite. Unless you get them for me, the postmaster will look like he got off easy."

"Brennan will kill me."

"If he don't, I will. Take you choice, Jenson."

Olaf Jenson said, "I'll get the dynamite. No, I don't carry it in my store. Chripes, I don't want to be blown to smithereens, Kimlock. It's cached in a cave back in the west hills."

"We'll ride out there together. Convenient for me, it bein' out west—'cause I'm ridin' that direction. My uncle's ranch is west, ain't it?"

"Five miles, due west. Jes' foller the river upstream. The cache is two miles outa town."

"Where's your horse?"

"Shed, behin'."

They went out the back door. Soon both rode out of Stirrup City. "Trail runs along the river through the timber," Jenson said.

Luke Kimlock shook his head. "You might ride in the brush, Jenson, but I don't. I take the ridge there."

Jenson paled. "Ambush?"

"Easy for a rider to whip ahead, hidden by the buckbrush. Then he'd light an' build his nest."

"I ride high with you," Jenson said. "Only one thing wrong about bein' up higher, though —you can skyline yourself an' draw bullets from below."

49

Luke Kimlock shrugged. "Man can't avoid all the danger in this life. Learned that fast years ago when I hired out as a mere kid to the Texas Rangers."

Jenson looked at him. "You sound old, Kimlock, but I bet you ain't seen twenty-eight yet."

Kimlock's eyes searched the rugged terrain below. Olaf Jenson rode ahead of him. The man packed no side arm nor did a rifle ride in his saddle holster.

Kimlock got the impression that although the merchant feared him, he respected him for standing up against Brennan and Stebbins. The middle-aged matron's words had given him the same impression.

He wondered if Stirrup City citizens wouldn't quickly rise up against the pair if they thought a chance lurked of their winning. It was an idea to play upon and maybe enlarge, Luke Kimlock reasoned.

"You got a family, Jenson?"

"Woman an' six kids. Four girls, two boys. Why ask?"

"You happy seein' them live in a town without law, where a rifle speaks an' a man is shot dead from his horse right in broad daylight on the town's main street?"

Jenson said nothing.

"Nice for kids to look at," Luke Kimlock said.

Jenson finally said, "I see your point, Kimlock, but when a town is controlled by guns—an' fear—An' one man alone, Kimlock, cain't do much of nothin', can he?"

"Wonder where Brennan an' Stebbins came from? I heard they rode into town together about two years ago. Bought the saloon and a bank so they had to have money."

"You're not the only one who thinks about that."

"Nobody knows where they come from, huh?"

"Nobody but them, Kimlock, an' they ain't tellin'. But they rid horses bearin' the Long X brand."

"Yeah. Where was the brand located on their critters?"

"Right shoulder. Small brand. Wire brands, I think. I remember clear. I wondered at such a small brand. Later I learned you could heat a wire an' make jus' such a brand."

Kimlock stored that. The Long X was a

North Texas iron, but other territories might have long X brands, too. But it was worth remembering.

"Here's my cache," Jenson said.

The dynamite was stored in a cave carved back into a small hill. Only a heavy wooden door marked its location. A thick copper padlock hung closed on a strong hasp.

"My uncle's ranch," Kimlock suddenly asked. "Why do Brennan and Stebbins want it?"

"Railroad, of course. Rails are going right up the river. Right across your uncle's spread, practically in his front yard. But they own it now, you know."

"They told me in town my uncle still occupies the house."

"Yeah, I heard the same. Him an' a few of his ol' hands are holed up inside. There's been some shootin', I hear, from the outside— Brennan an' Stebbins men. But I'm talkin' too much. Not another word, Kimlock. Here's six sticks of black powder."

Kimlock looked at the dynamite. Dynamite was something he knew little about. He'd bought it on a hunch, nothing more but many times his hunches turned out correctly.

"Caps are inside," Jenson said. "All you got to do is light the fuse—an' get out fast."

"How much?"

Jenson told him. Luke Kimlock paid. They went out, Jenson locking the door, then testing the big padlock.

"Brennan's liable to raise hell with me for this," the storeman said. "But you had a gun on me all the way, remember?"

Luke Kimlock smiled. He liked this man. "Later on I'll buy you a new window, Jenson. Good luck."

Jenson smiled tightly. "I'll need it." He swung into saddle and loped east toward Stirrup City, still threading the high ridge. Luke Kimlock watched until the man was out of sight in a depression.

Dynamite under his shirt, Kimlock mounted and rode west, thinking that if maybe a bullet hit him in the belly there'd sure be a grand and final explosion.

Quarter Circle V's ranch-buildings hugged the west bank of Stirrup River, built just high enough to escape spring's flood waters. The building closest to the river was an old log barn.

That noon the barn suddenly exploded. A loud roar shook the cottonwood trees and other

53

buildings. The old building flew skyhigh. Logs went high, then floated this way, then that.

Then, tired of suspension, they crashed down on the other buildings. Circle Diamond gunhands had made Quarter Circle V's bunkhouse their fortress. Timbers fell across the bunkhouse's sod roof.

The gunmen ran for the brush, the bunkhouse between them and the long log house, where Uncle Cy Blunt and his gunmen were located. What had happened, anyway?

They did not see Luke Kimlock approach the back door of the ranch-house, a bloody, gun-beaten sentry staggering ahead, but Uncle Cy, lying on a bed near the back window, did see him approach, and the old Texan gave out a Red River whoop that shook the old rafters.

"By gorry, my nephew, Luke Kimlock! An' a Brennan–Stebbin man, ahead—all beat up, an' bloody!"

The old timer tried to get out of the bed. He couldn't make it, for pain held him down. He beat the covers with gnarled fists.

"I'm goin' to kill 'em both!" he said.

"What two?" the ranch halfwit asked.

Uncle Cy Blunt glared at him. "General

Grant and his brother, of course, Wobbly Head."

"Didn't know the general had a brother," the halfwit said.

5

THAT evening the halfwit forgot. He lit a kerosene lamp. A bullet whammed in through a window already shot free of glass.

The bullet shot the wick assembly off the lamp's base. Kerosene ran over the table, immediately aflame. Luke Kimlock grabbed a blanket from Uncle Cy's easy-chair. He threw it over the flame. The blanket smothered it to death.

Another shot came. Flames had outlined Kimlock. The bullet tore into the far wall, missing a Quarter Circle V waddy by a few inches.

Uncle Cy's cane shot out, hooking the halfwit by his ankles. A harsh pull, and the halfwit was down on the floor, wondering what had happened.

"You do somethin' like that ag'in," Uncle Cy said, "an' I bran' you an' earmark you after I cut you, Wobbly."

"I ain't no bull calf."

"You'd be a steer when I got done with you."

Kimlock said, "That was a rifle shot, Uncle Cy. Too sharp, too clean, an' it sang like a rifle lead."

"Damn' near plugged me," a waddy said.

"Thet was the last lamp in the house," Uncle Cy said. "All t 'others been shot to smithereens, nephew. An' we're almost out of grub, too. What'd we do next?"

Darkness hid Luke Kimlock's smile. "I reckon I've done all I can, Uncle. I knocked Brennan on his rump. I sent Concho into the Happy Huntin' Grounds. The postmaster is still tryin' to clean the ink off'n his mug. I saw Deacon Stebbins shoot O'Rourke dead off a horse. An' I met a right purty girl."

"Who was she?"

"Miss Mary Burnett." Kimlock paused. "Maybe she isn't a miss. Dang my buttons, I never looked to see if she had a weddin' ring."

"She ain't married," a cowboy said.

"You oughta know," Uncle Cy growled. "How many times you proposed marriage to her, Curley?"

"Only eight, actual count."

"She evidently doesn't want to marry you," Luke Kimlock said. "This is a damn nice hunk

57

of high-grassed ranged here, Uncle Cy. I might make up my mind to stop lawin' aroun' an' settle here."

"I got a hunch Brennan an' Stebbins would like to help you do that," Uncle Cy said, and added, "Under six feet of sod, nephew. What'd we do next?"

"Your misery, not mine."

Uncle Cy said, "Hell of a kinfolk you turned out to be. You don't remember me raisin' you, huh? You'd still bee in that Matador jail fer beatin' up on the town marshal if'n my money hadn't bailed you out, young man."

"Let's get some facts straight," Luke Kimlock said. "You were ambushed last Wednesday between here an' Stirrup City."

Uncle Cy recited facts between groans. He'd been shot from a horse in the buckbrush, the bullet hitting him in the right shoulder. "Knocked me plumb off'n ol' Smoke hoss, nephew. Lucky Wobbly Head was with me. He got me back to the ranch."

"He sure went flyin' from leather," Wobbly Head said. "Jes' like a bird, I tell you." He looked about in the darkness.

"Right afore that—that afternoon—Neefy rode out an' tol' you that Stebbins an' Brennan had gone to the county seat—Beaverton—an' had gained ownership of your iron, huh?" Kimlock asked.

"That's right, nephew."

Luke Kimlock scowled. "Let's get somethin' straight, Unc. Your cowmen run over hundreds of square miles of range an' usually you ain't got deeds to a foot of it—it all belongs to Uncle Sam and is open to homesteaders. Jus' what land have you got deed to, if any?"

Suddenly rifle fire sounded from the Quarter Circle V guard on the porch. "You get the sonofabitch?" Uncle Cy asked.

"I believe I clipped him. He staggered outa sight, though, so it's hard to tell in this darkness."

"Better huntin' come shortly," the old Texan said. "Moon'll come up roun' an' bright. Where was we, nephew?"

Luke Kimlock repeated his question. Uncle Cy had homesteaded and proven up on the land his ranch buildings stood on. "Got three hundred an' twenty acres here—homestead an' hill-claim."

"You have deeds to any other land aroun' here?"

"Yeah, sure have. Two years ago put some

thirty cowpunchers on homesteads. Fact is, I own almost all the lan' on both sides of the river atween here an' Stirrup City, five miles."

"Cowpunchers proved up, then sold rights to you?"

"That's the deal. Railroad'll have to swing far north or south after leavin' Stirrup City or pay me what I ask for the right-of-way." The old Texan winced. "An' now Stebbins an' Brennan own it, not me."

"How could they get hol' of it?" Luke Kimlock asked. "You sell it to them?"

"Hell, no. I wouldn't give them two bastards the time of the clock! They went to their buddy thieves in thet courthouse in Beaverton an' got me declared incapable of handlin' my own affairs due to my age—an' now they own the whole sheebang."

"They get the titles transfered?"

"They sure did. Neefy had a copy of the paper. He left it here. You can read for yourself. You must know a little bit about legal affairs, havin' served so many arrest warrants an' such things while you was a lawman."

Wobbly Head opened a drawer. "Here it is, nephew."

Luke Kimlock took the paper. "I ain't your nephew," he corrected.

"That's right," the halfwit said. "You're Uncle Cy's nephew. I always look upon your uncle as my dad, so that'd make you my brother."

Luke Kimlock said, "A man can't win."

Squatting in a far corner, Luke Kimlock lit a sulphur and, in its flare, he hurriedly scanned the legal-looking document. The match died. He handed the paper back to Wobbly Head.

"You got enemies in the court house in Beaverton, uncle?"

"Ain't got no friends, 'pears like. They're regularly elected officials—you can buy each an' every one off with enough dough, an' I guess Stebbins an' Brennan paid them more than I'd have."

"Wonder where them two bastards come from?" Wobbly Head asked. "Nobody seems to know a thing about where they was an' what they did afore they hailed in here loaded with money a coupla years back."

Luke glanced at the halfwit. In the short time he'd been in this log ranch house he'd noticed that more than once or twice the presumably

61

feeble minded young cowpoke had come up with an interesting question or conclusion.

He had a hunch Wobbly Head was not as loco as some thought.

"Be interestin' to fin' out," Luke said, "an' it could be done easy enough. Telegram out of Beaverton on the railroad line. I guess I got everythin' clear now. You haven't got much grub here, huh?"

"'Nuf for a coupla days, no more," Uncle Cy said. "An' I cain't figure out no way to escape, nephew. Them Circle Diamon' rats has got us completely surrounded. If'n you hadn't had black powder, you'd never got in."

"Black powder can get us out," Luke Kimlock said.

Uncle Cy asked, "How?"

"Blast the sonsofguns skyhigh. They got no mercy on you. Who'd you figure shot you from the brush?"

"Never saw hide or hair of him," Uncle Cy said. "Buckbrush was mighty thick. An' out of it come lead—"

"Only you an' Wobbly Head?" Luke Kimlock asked.

"Jes' us two. He follers me like a dog. I picked him up when he was a homeless button

62

back in Omaha, Nebrasky. Was there with some cows to sell. You was ramroddin' the law then down in Laredo."

"Been some time ago, then," Luke pointed out. "How many shots was fired?"

"By the ambusher or by Wobbly Head?"

"I shot six times," Wobbly Head said. "My Winchester. But I reckon I hit only air 'cause we heard hoofs beatin' out damn fast afterwards."

"I mean by the ambusher," Luke Kimlock said.

"Jes' one, nephew. Knocked me from saddle, like Wobbly Head said."

Luke spoke to Wobbly Head. "What did you see, boy?"

Wobbly Head didn't answer immediately. He just sat and stared into the dark, apparently disregarding the question, and it was so dark Luke could not clearly see the youth's face.

Silence held the dark room. Cowboys hunkered by windows, rifles at the ready. One shifted, boot scraping the worn floor. They'd turned loose the Circle Diamond man Luke had pistol whipped.

The man had run across the yard toward the bunkhouse, bullets hammering dust around him. He'd skidded around the building's corner, Quarter Circle V hands laughing at his zigzagging tactics.

"I asked a question, remember?" Luke Kimlock shot the words at Wobbly Head.

"I never saw the ambusher. Like Uncle Cy says the bresh was too thick an' too high—but I figger it was only one man, brother Luke."

Luke grinned. BROTHER now, not NEPHEW? "Amen," he intoned. "Now, let's get the hell outa here, huh?"

"Suits me," Uncle Cy said.

Luke Kimlock sniffed the air. "This place stinks. Bachelor headquarters, nothin' ever washed. How much you figger this house is worth, Uncle Cy?"

"What're you drivin' at, nephew?"

Everybody listened.

"Wonderful location," Luke Kimlock continued. "Cottonwood trees, boulders, but these log buildings—they ain't much. They disgrace the location."

Uncle Cy asked angrily, "Could you build better?"

"I sure could."

"Where I trailed longhorns into this kentry I wasn't loaded down with money," the old

64

cowman said. "Beef was almost worthless. Garfield's depression had cowmen ridin' with bare feet in stirrups. I did the best I could."

Luke Kimlock squatted beside a guard and peered out the corner of the window. "I reckon Circle Diamon' men hang out around the bunkhouse, eh?"

"Right, Luke."

Luke Kimlock studied the log buildings. Light glowed from the windows. The bunkhouse, too, was made of native cottonwood logs.

And cottonwood didn't make good log buildings, Luke knew. Cottonwood logs were crooked and had knots.

When a man built a log building, he needed straight pine or spruce for logs. They fit flat against one another and needed only mud chinking to build a good wall.

Wobbly Head hunkered beside Luke.

Luke said, "That log shack left of the bunkhouse a few feet—the one closest to his house? What's it, Wobbly Head?"

"The tool shed, brother Luke."

Luke Kimlock scowled, rubbed his jaw reflectively. Whiskers grated. He needed a shave.

A bullet whistled through a window. Everybody ducked but Luke, who had his eyes on the tool shed.

"Let's say a man is on the roof of this house, Wobbly Head. Any way for him to get onto the roof of the tool shed?"

"What'd you aim to do, nephew?" Cy Blunt asked.

Luke paid his uncle no attention.

"They's a ladder on the south end of this house," Wobbly Head said. "They's an openin' to the roof in the south bedroom. Uncle Cy built a trap door into the roof, there."

"Makes it easy to get up on the roof an' cut down the weeds that grow in the sod," Uncle Cy said. "But what do you aim to do, nephew?"

"I'm not yet sure," Luke Kimlock said.

"A man can lay the ladder from this roof to the other," Wobbly Head said, "an' if he wants, the ladder acrost to the roof of the bunkhouse."

"You're sure the ladder's still there?"

"It's still there," a cowpuncher said. "I saw it this afternoon when I sat guard by the window there."

"Where's there a buggy?" Luke Kimlock asked. "Or a spring wagon, a democrat, a wagon—anything with wheels?"

"What'd you want that for?" Uncle Cy asked.

"To move you in," Luke said.

"Move me? I ain't goin' nowhere!"

"You sure of that?" Luke asked.

Uncle Cy had no answer. Wobbly Head said, "Wagon-shed's south in the bresh, brother Luke. The lumber wagon is busted but they's a buggy there—good shape, too."

"Where are there some horses to hitch to this buggy?" Luke spoke to Wobbly Head.

"All in the barn except your buckskin, an' you said you had him hid in the bresh."

Luke looked at the log barn. "We could never get a team—or a horse—out of there. They're watchin' the barn extra close, I'd say —figurin' we'll make a run for horses. What's this buggy got, tongue or shafts?"

"Shafts. Single horse used to pull it."

"One thing in our favor, but the buckskin's never been between shafts before. He might kick an' buck."

"He ain't got no harness, either," Wobbly Head said.

Luke nodded reflectively. "We can get aroun' that. Tie the shafts to the saddle's stirrups. Cut the saddle-strings loose, use them to tie. Can you navigate under your own power, Uncle Cy?"

67

"I can do anythin' to escape this trap."

Luke pulled away from the window, Wobbly Head following suit. "Okay, let's get movin'," Luke said. "You're my powder monkey, Wobbly Head."

"What'd you mean by thet, brother Luke?"

"You tote the dynamite."

"I don't like that one bit," Wobbly Head said, "but seein' you're the boss, I'll do as you order."

"You'd better."

Soon both were in the high sunflowers and weeds growing on the house's sod roof, creeping toward the ladder, with Wobbly Head gently holding the sticks of powder against his belly, trembling at each forward movement. Finally, they came to the roof's edge.

Luke peered into the darkness. He could see no ladder. His heart sank. The ladder had been removed. All depended on the ladder.

"Over there," Wobbly Head whispered. "To your left. Hid in the shadows, brother Luke."

Luke then saw the ladder. The top rung was quite a distance below the eave of the roof. Was his reach that long?

He crept toward the ladder, glad for the

protective high weeds. Suddenly a bullet whined overhead.

He went belly down fast. Overhead steel hit steel. Uncle Cy's prize weather vane suddenly toppled.

"Took it down the first shot," a voice said from the bunkhouse. "Even in this darkness, I did it."

The voice held pride.

Wobbly Head whispered, "Man, that was shootin', brother Luke!"

"Lots of luck."

They lay flat on their bellies, waiting a while. No more bullets came. Luke gingerly reached down for the ladder, fingers searching—and finding nothing.

"Where the hell—"

His sentence died unfinished. His fingers had found the ladder. He couldn't reach the top rung. He pulled the ladder slowly up by an upright two-by-six.

He worked carefully, silently. Finally, the ladder lay in the weeds, and Luke Kimlock wiped sweat from his forehead.

They snaked the long ladder through the roof-weeds. They laid it carefully across to the tool-shed's roof. Luke grabbed Wobbly Head's wrist, stopping the youth.

"All clear, boy?"

"Clear, brother Luke."

"Repeat, please."

Wobbly Head said quietly, "I'm the lightest. If you went across the ladder with your weight it would break."

"Good so far."

"I cross the ladder. I get on the tool-shed's roof. I pull the ladder in behind me. I lay it from the tool-shed to the bunkhouse."

"Good."

"I get on the bunkhouse's roof. I move through the weeds until I'm directly over the door. I then light a stick of dynamite. I drop it right in front of the door."

"Right."

"That keeps Circle Diamon' gunmen from runnin' out the door. They have to climb outa windows to escape. I pull out pronto. I drop one stick lighted on the bunkhouse roof."

"Good boy."

"Then I run back to the tool shed. I cross to the house roof, where we are now. Then I drop a stick on its roof." The boy paused. "I don't like havin' to blow up my home."

"We'll build a new one later. A good house, boy. You know what to do. Now, go ahead."

"Hope the boys can get Uncle Cy out an' into the buggy an' have your buckskin hitched up in time. Uncle Cy means the world to me. He took me off the streets an'—"

"I know. I wish that ladder would hold my weight, an' I'd do this—but it won't, so let's go, brother."

BROTHER? Luke grinned. He liked this boy. He now had the BROTHER habit?

"Wish me luck," Wobbly Head said.

"Luck, amigo."

Squatting on the roof, hidden by high sunflowers and weeds, Luke watched the boy cross the ladder—a dark shadow in darkness. No bullets came. The ladder left the house's roof. It snaked across to the tool shed's roof.

Luke's heart beat heavily. His eyes probed the darkness, seeing nothing until a match flared in the weeds on the bunkhouse's roof.

The match died. A fine line of fire fell from the roof to land on the ground in front of the door.

Men screamed from inside the bunkhouse. Luke stood up, short gun in hand. Fear for the boy struck him. What if the powder exploded

71

prematurely? What if the boy couldn't make it back in time?

It seemed an eon of time ran by before the ladder's end was poked the roof's direction. He caught it, anchored it on the sod roof; Wobbly Head scrambled across.

"I'll blow up the house," Luke said. "You drop off the south side. Fast, now—I'll be right with you."

"Okay, brother."

Wobbly Head disappeared over the ridge beam. Luke dropped his dynamite down the chimney, thinking that if the cowhands hadn't got Uncle Cy out by now it would be goodby Uncle Cy.

Then, he too dropped to the ground. Wobbly Head waited. Luke glanced into a window. The big living room was without occupants. Relief hit him. Uncle Cy and the rest had made it to the buggy.

North beyond the house came a heavy roar. Logs and timbers suddenly floated skyward in scarlet, arching flame. The bunkhouse had blown up. Flames instantly took control of Quarter Circle V's other buildings.

The tool shed also went skyhigh. The forge had hot coals. They spread out high in the air like skyrockets. Some landed on the barn. The barn broke into flames.

Luke Kimlock and Wobbly Head sprinted south toward the trees and brush, Wobbly Head in the lead. They'd just reached the buggy when the house blew up with a mighty roar.

"What the hell—?" Uncle Cy snarled from the buggy seat. "You blow up my domiciles, too, you bastard?"

"Accident, Uncle," Luke Kimlock said, grinning.

Logs flew everywhere. One crashed into the crown of a nearby tree, bringing the crown crashing down. The buckskin didn't have time to rebel. Luke Kimlock leaped into his saddle, hit him with his spurs.

The brute lunged ahead, jerking the buggy so hard Uncle Cy's head almost popped from shoulders. The rig thundered east on the wagon road leading to Stirrup City, Quarter Circle V gunhands hanging on for dear life, Wobbly Head on the seat holding Uncle Cy steady.

No shots came. Circle Diamond men had fled north into the timber. Luke turned in saddle, looking back. Quarter Circle V was burning nicely, flames cutting the darkness.

"Where we goin'?" Uncle Cy hollered.

Luke Kimlock yelled back. "To hell, Uncle Cy, to hell!"

"We cain't go there. We've already been there. Dang your buttons, nephew, where are we headin' for?"

Luke Kimlock straightened in saddle. "You'd never guess," he hollered back.

6

THAT same afternoon Deacon Stebbins had sat beside his window looking down on Stirrup City's one and only street, occasionally lifting his violin to seek surcease from physical pain and his galling thoughts in savage music. Everything had gone wrong this day.

First, Luke Kimlock had got through the blockade. Small moment did it make that Kimlock had killed Concho. Concho didn't count. The thing that counted was that Kimlock was alive, not dead.

Then, Kimlock had knocked Brennan flying, plate-glass and all. And Brennan had a rep as a rough-and-tumble saloon fighter.

Deacon Stebbins raised his violin. He laid his jowl along the smooth wood. He played savagely, bow bouncing a bit of old Germanic music filled with hate and war and strife and death.

Sudden pain lanced along his spine. He winced as he lowered his violin. He closed his eyes. He fought pain. Finally the pain receded. Tears filled his eyes. He had unjustly earned this pain. The sins of the father—or the mother —he reasoned should not be laid upon their children.

But in his case, they had been. Or so Doc Miller claimed. It ran in the blood, the French pox, Doc Miller said. It broke out in descendants time and time again.

Deacon Stebbins silently cursed his parents although they were long dead, buried under New York sod. He breathed deeply.

Anger returned. That damned Tim O'Rourke —Figured all he had to do was ride out with Stebbins–Brennan money in his pocket—money he'd been paid to kill one Luke Kimlock. The money lay on the low table in front of him.

Deacon Stebbins leaned forward. One hundred dollars in half eagles. Twenty five dollar gold pieces. His long fingers lifted the gold, let it silently fall back into the pile.

Deacon Stebbins' twisted fingers pushed one half-eagle to one side. That would be Neefy's pay after he returned from boothill after burying O'Rourke and Concho.

Neefy . . . Again, the banker's thin lips twisted. Neefy had backed down in front of

Luke Kimlock. Neefy had turned the white feather.

Maybe just as well—Ambush was the best way. Had Neefy matched guns with Kimlock—killed Kimlock—townspeople might have been aroused too much. His gunning down O'Rourke from the bank's window had not been good policy, but rage had temporarily mastered sagacity.

He heard bootheels on the back stairway. For one moment, his blood froze; he reached out, snagging the Winchester .30–30 rifle leaning against the wall beside the window.

Luke Kimlock? Climbing to have it out with him? He cocked his small, bloodless head, listening. Then, he recognized the boot-sounds. Silver Brennan, heavy of tread; his guard, with a lighter tread.

He put the rifle back against the wall. A low voice sounded beyond the door.

"Silver, boss," the guard said.

"Let him in," Deacon Stebbins said.

The key grated. The door swung in. Silver Brennan entered, his right eye swollen shut, blue.

Deacon Stebbins said, "Sit down, Silver."

Brennan took a chair. He sat uneasily on its edge. "He's rough with his fists, Deacon."

"I saw it," the banker said. "You didn't have much chance."

"Chance, hell! I get the jump on him—like he did on me—an' we'll see who's the best man, banker!"

Deacon Stebbins' smile showed scepticism.

"I'll kill that sonofabitch yet!" Silver Brennan angrily said.

"Neefy's afraid of him."

"Kimlock swings a fast gun, Deacon. He's ramrodded some tough trail towns. O'Rourke asked him if he wasn't the Wyomin' Ranger who settled the Johnson County war by killin' Kid Peterson."

"I heard. Through the window." Deacon Stebbins' long forefinger idly plucked a violin string. "Damn lucky Fred Rudd intercepted his letter to his uncle. If Rudd hadn't, he'd have ridden in easier than he has done."

Silver Brennan laughed softly. "Fred Rudd, Stirrup City postmaster—Ah, you should see Fred now, Deacon. Kimlock rubbed Fred's face in ink. Fred's still got the blue stain. He sure looks comical."

Deacon Stebbins said, "Fred Rudd couldn't

look anything but comical. He was born looking comical. He's a freak to begin with. He'll die a freak. Then Kimlock made Olaf Jenson sell him dynamite, huh?"

"He sure did. Held a gun on Olaf, all the way to the powder cache. Olaf is still shiverin'. He claims he's never seen a man as cold-blooded a killer as Luke Kimlock."

"Jenson's not seen many men, then," the banker said.

"What'd you figger he aims to do with the dynamite?"

"Blow out some cottonwood stumps." Deacon Stebbins' cynicism broke through. Anger flushed Brennan's fist hammered face.

"You ain't funny, Deacon. All you have to do is sit up here safe an' watch. You ain't down below on the battlefield like Neefy an' me. Neefy an' me do the dirty work. Okay, you're so damn smart—what's our next move, banker?"

"Kill Luke Kimlock."

"We tried that. Right now Neefy's pattin' dirt down on Concho's dead mug."

Deacon Stebbins looked out the window. "If at first you don't succeed, try, try again," he intoned. "We got all sewed up legally. As long as Mike Hanna keeps his head down in the court house, we'll be all right."

"That's your end of the deal," Brennan said. "You do the thinkin' an' I do the orderin'. But when a man fools around with Uncle Sam he's takin' a dangerous chance."

"What do you mean?"

Brennan got to his feet. "For instance, that government homestead deed to Cy Blunt. Yeah, Mike Hanna's also US Land Commissioner for this area, besides workin' in the Recorder's office in Beaverton but don't forgit in Great Falls there's a boss over Hanna, the big head for Uncle Sam in the Territory of Montana, Deacon."

"You tell me nothing, Silver."

Brennan said, "It'd be different if we was dealin' with a stupid, ordinary cowpoke but this Luke Kimlock ain't that. He's lawed and he knows somethin' about how a county is run an' the legal angles of same."

"I've considered that."

"Okay, Deacon, okay. You've tied up all the loose ends. Now, in light of that, what's next?"

"Kill Luke Kimlock."

Brennan grinned. "Right back where we started. I'll order Neefy to kill him. From ambush or openly. Neefy gets the order. What if Neefy runs out, like O'Rourke tried to do?"

"We kill him, too."

"Who kills him?"

Deacon Stebbins' thin face showed anger. "Damn it, man, can't you get one thing through your thick skull? That money—the right amount—can buy anythin' a man wants?"

"You'd set a price on Neefy's head? If he tucks tail an' tried to run out?"

"A price just high enough to make it profitable for somebody to hunt him down and kill him."

"I'll order him," Brennan said.

Stebbins cocked his head. "Somebody coming in the alley," he said.

Silver Brennan listened. He heard not a sound but the wind softly singing in the bank's eaves. Then he heard the guard talking to somebody below. Soon the guard's footsteps and those of the visitor sounded outside on the stairway landing.

"Come in," Deacon Stebbins intoned. "Unlock the door, Silver, please."

Brennan turned the key. The guard's head came in. "Finn to see you, boss."

"Send him in."

Finn Williamson was a blonde, heavy-shouldered man of thirty. "If you're lookin' for Kimlock, boss, he's at Quarter Circle V headquarters."

"Alive or dead?" Deacon Stebbins asked.

"Plumb alive, an' kickin' well. Hell, he uses dynamite, he does."

Deacon Stebbins asked, "What'd you mean by that, Finn?"

"You mind that ol' log barn out there, settin' closest to the river? Well, about two hours ago that barn jes' suddenly exploded. Went up in logs which landed all over."

Brennan listened. Deacon Stebbins idly rubbed his glossy violin's back, eyes on the street below.

"And then what?" the banker asked.

"Well, us boys on guard rushed over there. From what I can make of it, the guard on the south side—George Harlem—he worked his way toward the bombin', an' smack dab somethin' comes down on his head, knockin' him silly."

Silver Brennan cursed. "I know the rest. Kimlock's pistol, huh? An' now Kimlock—an' Harlem—are in the house with the ol' uncle an' the other Quarter Circle V hands we had corraled?"

"That's the deal, Silver. Kimlock turned George loose. Beat him up good, then throw him out a window, glass an' all. The man's a savage, I tell you."

"This is a savage game," Deacon Stebbins said.

"That all, Finn?"

"Ain't it enough?"

"Too much," Stebbins said. Then, to Brennan, "Take him down to the saloon. Give him a few snorts and a bottle for the boys staked out around Quarter Circle V."

"What'll Kimlock be apt to do now?" Silver Brennan asked.

Deacon Stebbins sighed softly and said, "He's got a number of moves. We got enough hands out there, though. I'm glad I know where the bastard is. You can't kill a man when you don't know where he can be found. Good day, Silver. Same to you, Finn."

Silver Brennan's good eye narrowed. Deacon Stebbins was literally kicking him out of Deacon's quarters, but the saloon keeper said, "Let's make tracks, Finn."

Brennan and Finn Williamson left. Deacon

83

Stebbins listened to their bootheels pound down, hit the alley dust, then turn the alley's corner and die against the distance.

Then, bent almost double, using his rifle as a crutch, he went to the door, turned the key, and locked it. He experimented. He tried walking without the rifle's aid.

He almost fell forward. The rifle's barrel hit the floor in time to prevent his fall. He tried again. With supreme difficulty, he reached his chair. His thin face was wet with sweat.

He did not sit down. He braced himself against the back of the chair. He reached to his right. His broad gunbelt hung from a wooden peg. He took it free and attempted to strap it around his waist with one hand.

He couldn't do the chore. He needed to use both hands. Therefore he leaned against the chair. Fingers trembling, he finally had the belt buckled around his thin waist, heavy .45 flat against his lean hip.

He tied the strings down, anchoring the holster. Then he reached out and snagged a crutch from its resting place against the wall. He hefted it, then thought better, and restored the crutch to its old position.

His left hand went out, fingers gnarled claws.

They fastened around his rifle. Again, the rifle went under his left armpit as a crutch.

He breathed heavily from exertion, nostrils flaring. Then, weight on the rifle-butt, he hobbled from behind the chair to the middle of the room. He now faced his target on the north wall.

He'd had the target especially made for indoor gunslinging. A carpenter had built him a coffin-like box. This had been placed on end and filled with sand, then lidded shut.

Over this had been placed three single-bed mattresses, which in turn had been covered with heavy canvas—and on this canvas had been painted the image of a gunman.

The gunman was crouched, pistol poked out in front. Now, the banker faced this silent, deadly gunman, with Deacon Stebbins' weight on the rifle crutch.

The banker suddenly assumed a gunman's crouch. His right hand flashed down, smacked the gun-butt; the gun rose, firing from the hip.

Shiny metal chips had been pinned over the image's heart and forehead—two placed a half-inch apart over the heart, a single metal disk over the head's front.

Three times the big pistol belched flame and

lead. First the disk over the forehead disappeared. Then, one by one, the two disks over the heart went singing across the room.

Deacon Stebbins fired only three shots, all from the hip—and the three disks had been sent spinning. How he stood there, balanced on the rifle, a thin smile edging his thin lips.

Then, he scowled fiercely. His marksmanship pleased him; his speed of lifting, leveling, firing did not please him. Despite daily practice, he seemed unable to speed up his draw.

He practiced pulling his gun. Time and time again the .45 rose, leveled, steadied as he shot at the belly, the forehead, the chest. Outside, townspeople stopped, listened.

Mary Burnett said to the Greek, "Deacon Stebbins shooting that dummy again. Oh, that terrible man!"

"Practicin' up for that Kimlock fella," the Greek said. "Kimlock's as good as buried right now, if he's crazy enough to tangle with Stebbins."

"Don't be too sure, Alexander."

"Alexander ain't my name. My name is Giovanni."

Mary sighed. "How long have you been with me, Alex?"

86

The Greek studied her. "A little over two years. Why?"

"I ever so much as ever make the smallest invitation to you, Alex?"

"No. What're you drivin' at?"

"You'll find out. I've slapped your hands away a number of times. I believe I should pay you off and let you go."

"Why would you do that?"

"You think you own this cafe. At least, you act that way. You don't own it. I do. I got along before you wandered into town and I can get along just as well if you wandered out."

"Deacon Stebbins has asked me a coupla times to cook for his crew at his ranch. Silver Brennan wants me to cook in his saloon."

"I think that's a wonderful idea, Alex. Mrs. Jensen has asked a number of times to cook for me, seeing her children are all grown and gone."

Alex blinked. Apparently he hadn't expected Mary to take up his offer to leave. He realized he'd trapped himself. Deacon Stebbins hadn't promised him a job and neither had Brennan.

"Forget it," he said.

Mary Burnett hid her smile. "Just remember you work here and don't own here."

"I'll remember."

Mary went to the cafe's front. Deacon Stebbins' gun had been silent some minutes now. Mary knew that the guard was sewing up the holes in the painted gunman, a task he had after each practice session.

Mary looked up at the bank's second story. Deacon Stebbins could be seen hobbling to his chair, a rifle as a crutch. Mary saw him settle down. From his chair, Deacon Stebbins could watch Stirrup City.

Mary wondered where Luke Kimlock was. She liked Luke, she decided—in fact, Luke would make good husband material . . . that is, if he didn't get killed first. Mary smiled to herself. Mary Burnett wanted to marry and raise a family like other women her age.

She usually closed at eight in the evening unless late diners came in, and this night some railroad workers came in just before closing time. Railroad workers had money and spent money and business had not been at all good that day so Mary served them, Alex grumbling about their big orders of meat and spuds and all the trimmings.

The railroad workers were half drunk. They'd been consorting with the ladies over

Silver Brennan's bar and talked loudly of their various companions of a few minutes past, comparing the ability of one girl against another.

Their loud, lewd talk sickened Mary who locked the door to make sure no other customers could enter. The talk seemed to please Alexander, who stood in the kitchen doorway and listened.

Mary counted the till. Darkness held Stirrup City. Kerosene lamps glowed here and there. Noise came from Silver Brennan's saloon, as usual. Mary knew that many in Stirrup City considered the saloon and its red light upstairs a definite detriment to Stirrup City's progress.

Only yesterday the Methodist Ladies Aid women had discussed the saloon to some length, she'd learned.

She heard a rider lope fast into town. The man pulled his lunging bronc to haunches, left the saddle on the run, leaving his mount rein tied to the dusty street in front of the alley leading behind Deacon Stebbins' bank.

Mary noticed Stebbins' heavy drapes were drawn. Yellow lamplight glowed behind them. She'd recognized the rider as Sandy Malone, for she knew each and every rider who worked for Quarter Circle V or Circle Diamond.

Sandy Malone worked for the Stebbins—Brennan owned Circle Diamond. And Sandy had been in a terrible hurry to see his boss.

Alexander had moved in behind her. "Wonder what's goin' on? Maybe Circle Diamon's finally killed that Kimlock gent?"

For some reason, Mary Burnett's heart hit an extra beat. "Maybe you can find out, Alex?"

"I'm as curious as you are."

The Greek left. He came back just as Mary was closing the door behind the last railroad worker.

"Yeah, it was about Kimlock, sure as shootin'. Circle Diamon' had him an' his uncle an' some Quarter Circle V hands penned in the Quarter Circle V's home ranch."

"I already know that."

"Well, Kimlock an' his uncle an' his uncle's cowpunchers broke out of Quarter Circle V. Dynamited everything. Left the ol' buildin's burnin'."

"Where's Luke Kimlock now?"

The Greek laughed cynically. "You sound interested, Mary. Well, Kimlock an' Cy Blunt an' Quarter Circle V moved into Circle

Diamond's home ranch, an' they're settled smack-dab in the Stebbins—Brennan big stone house, they say."

"They occupy Stebbins' house?"

"That's the word. Gunned their way in. Holy lord, what an insult to Stebbins an' Brennan. Like slappin' a bull in the face with a red towel. The whole country'll be laughing at Brennan an' Stebbins!"

"Anybody get hurt?"

"Only ones I know of are Circle Diamon' han's at Quarter Circle V when the black powder went off. Couple of boys got hit by fallin' logs an' such stuff."

"How about when Kimlock an' his men took over Circle Diamond?"

"They jumped everybody there by surprise. I don't know all the details. I jus' was in the saloon. Sandy Malone went up to talk to Stebbins. Brennan was talkin' with Mike Hannigan who come in from Circle Diamon' with Sandy."

"I never saw Hannigan ride in. I only saw Sandy."

"Hannigan came into the saloon from the alley. That's why you never seen him. I'm goin' over an' try to learn more."

"Do that. And report back, please."

"There comes Sandy aroun' the corner now," the cook said. "He's left Stebbins an' is goin' for Brennan."

Sandy Malone hurried into Brennan's bar, the Greek hard on the cowpuncher's spur rowels.

Mary Burnett said a little prayer for Luke Kimlock's safety. She locked the door behind her, then smiled—what good was a lock with the glass front of the door knocked out?

Should she sleep in her cafe tonight to protect it? She smiled again. There was no money in the cafe's cash-box. She had it in the buckskin bag in her hand.

With the money gone, all to steal would be old crockery, pots and pans and silverware.

She unlocked the door.

At that moment, Sandy Malone and Silver Brennan left the saloon and hurried toward the alley leading to Deacon Stebbins' stairway, both men walking rapidly.

Malone's horse stood patiently waiting at the alley's mouth, ground-tied by his trailing bridle-reins. The horse had been ridden hard. His flanks rose and fell and sweat covered him.

Mary shook her head slowly. Cowpunchers

had little regard for horseflesh, she'd long ago
learned.

They rode with savage spurs, pounded with
shot loaded quirts, bloodied a horse's mouth
with cruel, choking spade-bits.

She called, "Sandy."

Sandy and Brennan turned. Sandy said,
"Yes, Miss Burnett?"

"Your good horse. He needs water and
curried. Why don't you take him to the livery-
barn? If you won't, I will."

Sandy looked inquiringly at Brennan.
Brennan said, "Do as the crazy woman wants,
Sandy. You've already talked to Stebbins."

"Okay, boss."

Brennan continued on to Stebbins' back
stairway. Sandy picked up his bronc's reins.

"Danged females," he said. "Always inter-
ferin' in a man's business. I'll be hanged if I'll
ever get married."

Mary Burnett smiled.

93

7

THAT same night Doc Henry Miller's boy couldn't find the prize Miller milk cow, an imported Holstein worth ten times the price of a range cow. The boy searched the brush up and down Stirrup River. Finally at ten he reported failure to his father.

"Wasn't Spotty with the town cows in the town pasture?" the doctor asked.

"She was there this afternoon. Sonny Brown saw her about six. Then when he went after the town cows about seven, she was gone."

"Was the fence down somewhere? Or the gate open?"

The boy shook his head. "I went aroun' the fence. It was all up, all three bobwires. An' Sonny said the gate was closed when he come for the cows. It's only got one gate, daddy."

"I don't understand it, son. Let's go look for Spot."

"Mama doesn't feel well. I gotta wash the dishes."

Doc Henry Miller left, mumbling about it

being a hell of a doctor who couldn't keep his own family well, but realizing his wife was a bundle of nerves—for who wouldn't be, living in a town where the town boss openly shot and killed a man on the street?

The town pasture was on Stirrup City's north end along the Stirrup River. To the doctor's surprise, the prize Holstein stood at the quarter-section's far fence, close to the timber, and, as he got closer, he saw the cow was tied by a rope around her neck to a cottonwood tree.

"What the hell—?"

A man walked out of the buckbrush at that moment. He carried a level .45 pistol. "How are you, doc?"

"Luke Kimlock!"

"I took your cow across the river and hid her in the brush. I wanted you to come in person to look for her."

"Why?"

"I want you to ride out and give medical attention to my uncle."

"I can't do it, Kimlock. They'll kill me."

"If you don't go with me, I'll kill you."

Doctor Henry Miller studied the tall cowpuncher. Finally he said, "By hell, you would. You're a cold blooded man, Luke

95

Kimlock. Brennan and Stebbins will have a hard time eliminating you."

"They've already had that and they'll have more. Where do you want to die, Doc?"

"I don't want to die."

"You will if you don't come with me. Either way, you're in a bind, man. I doubt if Brennan an' Stebbins would dare kill you. You're the town doc, even if you are a rat and a doc always has a bit of respect, even one as low as you."

"Thanks."

"Make up your mind, doc—and fast. Either you die here or in Brennan's saloon. Or maybe Stebbins will shoot you down in plain view like he did to that O'Rourke skunk?"

"I'll take a chance. I'll go with you."

"Good."

"Heard you moved into Circle Diamond, right under their noses. Kimlock, you hit them hard, then. Stebbins looks on that ranch like a millionaire looks on his only son. They spent a small fortune on those stone buildings. I doubt if they'll blow them up like you boys blew up Cy's spread. Too much money involved. My bag is in my office."

"Let's go get it. Down the alley, doc."

"We got to go past Stebbins' guard."

"We'll swing around him. Night's gettin' pretty dark."

"What if I holler to him?"

"It'll be your last yelp, an' his too if he comes after us."

"Jus' jokin', Kimlock."

They reached the door without trouble. Doc Miller went inside and seemed to stay a long time. Luke entered the office. Doc Miller was just ready to leave, black bag in hand.

"What took you so long?"

"Looked for some special medicine for gunshot wounds. Had it in my desk but couldn't find it right away. A man has to watch against tetanus with gunshots, you know."

"That's a fancy name for lockjaw, ain't it?"

"Right. Tetanus kills more gunshot victims than the bullet itself does. That's what killed Marshal Jake Raleigh over in Broken Bow, Nebraska."

"I knew Jake," Luke Kimlock said. "He was a good lawman. What's this comin'?"

With a sweep of his right arm, Luke Kimlock sent the medico back into the office. He stepped inside, closed the door. Boots approached in the night. Luke Kimlock heard a man and woman

97

talking. The pair stopped in the alley just outside the door.

The man said, drunkenly, "Martha, I got a little shack on the edge of town. We kin sleep together there tonight, darlin'."

"No we can't. I got to work out of my crib. If Silver Brennan even knew I sneaked out with you, Joe, he'd skin my ass an' ship me out— an' I'm makin' money here, with the railroad crew comin' in about every night. I turned four tricks just this afternoon at two bucks a trick. Hell, you know—I gave you half the money."

"I remember, darlin'. Then why don't we do it in your room?"

"Not unless you wanna pay, Joe. Brennan's madame collects at the head of the stairs. An' she don't know about me an' you. An' if she did you'd still have to pay."

"Ain't no justice," the man said.

The pair walked on, still talking. Finally the alley was quiet. Luke Kimlock and Doc Miller left.

Luke Kimlock had his buckskin and another saddled horse hidden in high brush slightly east of Stirrup City. Doc Miller complained that the stirrup leathers were adjusted too long. He couldn't get his feet in stirrups. "I don't want to bounce around like a jack-in-a-box."

"Put your boots between the leathers just above the stirrups," Luke Kimlock said.

"I got them there now, but now my knees are bent too much."

"Oh, to hell with it," Luke said. "Give me your bag. Bounce to your heart's content. Do you good. You've bounced to the orders of Brennan an' Stebbins ever since they hailed into town, my uncle told me."

"What else could I have done? You want me killed?"

"Not right now," Luke Kimlock said, "but after you treat my uncle."

"Ain't no justice."

Luke grinned in the dark. "That's what that pimp said back in the alley, remember."

Doc Miller remained silent. Circle Diamond's head ranch was four miles east of Stirrup City, its fine buildings also located on the south bank of Stirrup River in the cottonwood trees.

"I take it your uncle's in the house?" Doc Miller said.

"That he is," Luke Kimlock assured.

"How'd Quarter Circle V get into Circle Diamond's headquarters?"

99

"Same way we got out of Quarter Circle V. With flame and explosions. I sneaked into Circle Diamon' along the river's timber. I blew up a blacksmith shop. While the Circle Diamon' hands come runnin', we moved in from the opposite direction. We were inside before they knew what happened."

"Any of them wounded?"

"A couple were shot. We saw them fall. Others came out under a white flag an' drug them into the bunkhouse. Any come to town to you for treatment?"

"Not a one. You must have killed them."

"Be nice if we did. Good riddance. I'm almost out of black powder. I'll have to kidnap Olaf Jenson again. Or raid his cache myself, seein' I know now where it is."

"Stebbins ate out Olaf. Said he'd kick him outa the hardware store. Stebbins an' Brennan own the buildin', you know. Olaf got purty lippy. He called both of them some names. He'd not dared do that before you an' your gun came into this territory."

"I hope more join him," Luke Kimlock said. "Well, here we are. You tell Stebbins—an' Brennan, too—that if they harm a hair on Olaf's head I'm killin' them both."

Doc Miller laughed. "They kinda figure you aim to do just that anyway, Kimlock."

Luke Kimlock drew rein. Kerosene lamps lit in various Circle Diamond buildings ahead north showed yellow through the timber. "Here we are. Get off'n that cayuse. Here's your bag."

"How we gonna get into the house? Hell, I don't wanna get gutshot, Kimlock. I'm only forty seven, too damn young to die."

"You stay here. I'll be right back."

Doc Miller sat down. Thus, he was hidden in buckbrush. "I'll not move a step," he said. "I mean it. I fear you more than I do Brennan an' Stebbins."

"I'm glad to hear that."

Luke Kimlock disappeared in the night. Doc Henry Miller sat and thought. This thing was getting serious. And dangerous. He wasn't afraid of Deacon Stebbins. He had Deacon right where he wanted him.

Deacon had called in other pioneer doctors. From Beaverton, Hangton, Great Falls, Billings. He'd even traveled east for medical attention. None of these doctors had done Deacon a bit of good.

Doc Miller knew the Deacon. The Deacon had a great pride. You played up to his pride and you had Deacon Stebbins under your spell, especially if you were a medical doctor.

Doc Miller knew that most people were awed by medical doctors, just as they were awed by priests. Most thought a doctor knew the answers to all questions. A smart doctor didn't try to change their opinions. He gloried in the spotlight of importance.

Doc Miller knew that the greater part of curing was in flattery of the patient. He concocted a brew of sagebrush leaves, bull-berries, dried chokecherries and, in this, he put at least forty percent grain alcohol which he had freighted in from Minneapolis in five-gallon tins.

Deacon Stebbins claimed Doc Miller's medicine was the best, helping him the most. He couldn't smell the grain alcohol or taste it in the vile smelling, vile tasting brew.

Doc Miller knew the alcohol kept Deacon Stebbins half drunk most of the time, a fact the Deacon himself wasn't aware of. Deacon Stebbins said the only doctor who'd ever helped him was Doc Henry Miller.

Therefore Deacon Stebbins wasn't going to shoot the only man who helped him ease his pain, and Doc Miller knew this.

Within five minutes, Luke Kimlock returned, a stumbling figure ahead of him, Luke's pistol in the man's back.

"Let's move, Doc," Luke Kimlock said.

The moon was now rather bright. "That's Lew Stokes," Doc Miller said. "He works for the Deacon and Brennan."

"He wasn't much of a guard," Luke said. "Get movin' toward the house, you two. You first, Doc. Then you, Stokes. With my gun in your back, Stokes. Holler to your fellow gunmen that if one shoots at me I'll kill you with a bullet through your spine."

"What if one shoots at me?" Doc Miller asked.

"That's your lookout," Luke Kimlock said. "Get movin' toward the house, men."

The big stone house lay ahead in moonlight. When they got to the clearing surrounding the house Lou Stokes hollered, "He's behin' me but he's got his gunsight right against my backbone. Don't shoot 'cause he'll shoot me in two if you do, men."

There was no answer. A nighthawk zoomed noisely in, hunting mosquitos—of which there were millions. The bird's wings whistled as he flew away. The house had no lights.

A voice from a window said, "We're pertectin' you, Luke. We see a move out there an' we're shootin', an' not to miss."

"Good boy, Tony."

They went toward the back door. It opened before them, then closed behind them. Later that night, Doc Henry Miller supplied details to a hunched over Deacon Stebbins, there above the bank.

Neefy lounged on a settee, gun moved around to be close at hand. Silver Brennan squatted on his bootheels, broad muscular back against the wall. Lamplight glistened on his gun-handle.

Doc Miller told the trio about his milk cow's disappearance. "Kimlock set a trap. He put a gun in my back. The man is savage. He's a killer. He'd have shot my spine in two."

Deacon Stebbins waved a claw impatiently. "We know that. What did you learn? How bad is ol' Cy Blunt wounded? How many men they got there? What they got in line of weapons?"

"He's not in bad shape. That is, unless infection sets in, and I doubt if it will. I didn't get to count all their hands. Some were in other rooms watchin' windows."

Deacon Stebbins said, "That wonderful house and its costly furniture, all hand-made in

Great Falls. And those bastards with their spurs gougin' those table tops, those desks—"

Brennan said, "An' that ain't all. We had a damn big cache of guns an' ammunition in that house. Wonder if they found the cache?"

"They couldn't miss findin' it," Deacon Stebbins said. "You hear anything from them in that ammunition line, Doc?"

"They found it. Ol' Cy told me to be sure and thank you for the pistols, the rifles, the shotguns and all that ammunition. Made a point to make sure I'd not forget."

Neefy said not a word. Neefy listened. Neefy realized that, with the coming of Luke Kimlock, this had turned into a real war. Tim O'Rourke had been right. O'Rourke had wanted nothing to do with Luke Kimlock.

Neefy wondered if he didn't feel now the way O'Rourke had felt this afternoon.

Neefy kept on listening, remaining silent.

"They'd be tough to blast out," Doc Miller said. "When you got done, they might be dead —but that nice bunch of ranch building wouldn't be standing up. It'd be done, burning."

"He still got dynamite?" Brennan asked.

"While I was at the ranch, Kimlock an' the

105

halfwit raided Jenson's cache, cleaned it out. They held me prisoner until they came back 'cause they were afraid I might tell you men."

Brennan smiled thinly. "Well, that's that, Deacon. We can't blow them out with black powder unless we go east an' get some from the railroad boys dynamitin' them cuts."

Deacon Stebbins shook his head. "We aren't blastin' down our own buildings. There are other ways!"

"Like what?" Brennan asked.

Deacon Stebbins waved his hand. "Tomorrow's another day. Let me do a little thinkin', men. Our men at the ranch, Doc— any of them get killed in the fight?"

"I don't know. They wouldn't tell me. Kimlock came in behin' Stokes, slugged him cold, then threw him in the root cellar an' locked the door."

Brennan grinned. "He won't get out of there unless they let him. We made those rock an' concrete walls two feet thick to keep out the heat an' cold."

"Any others in the cellar?" Deacon Stebbins asked.

Doc Miller got to his feet. "I don't know. They were awful close-mouthed. They told me only what they wanted you an' Brennan to know, Deacon."

Deacon Stebbins nodded.

"I'd best get home," the doctor said. "Wife ain't feelin' well."

Brennan grinned. "She's sick all the time, to hear you say it. She's forty, at least. Time to trade her in on two twenties, Doc."

"Where'll I get them?"

"Upstairs, over my saloon."

Deacon Stebbins said shortly, "Enough of that. That kind of talk don't count. You were at Circle Diamond, Doc. You missed a bet."

Doc Miller stopped at the door. "And that, Deacon?"

"You could have fixed medicine with a little somethin' in it that would have shoved ol' Cy over the ridge."

"I thought of that."

"Then why didn't you?"

Doc Miller shrugged.

"You had the junk in your bag, didn't you?"

"I just couldn't do it, Deacon."

"Get out," Deacon Stebbins ordered.

Doc Miller left. Brennan rose. He spoke to Neefy. "We'd best drag out. Deacon's ready to blow his cinch!"

Neefy left, bootheels pounding. Brennan stopped, looked at Deacon Stebbins. "We gotta get that ol' man outa the picture. With him alive that will we got off him the day he was ambushed could be contested in court, couldn't it?"

"It sure could be."

"Where's the will now?"

"Downstairs. In my safe. Where'd you think somethin' that important would be?"

Brennan eyed the banker coldly. "You can get lippy with the others, Deacon, but not with me," he warned. "It could have been left with the clerk and recorder down in Beaverton."

"He didn't have it long. Only long enough to make a copy."

"He copy it by hand?"

Deacon Stebbins shook his head. "You're way behind time, friend. Records don't copy no more. They all make photographs."

Brennan rubbed his jaw. "I sure hope to hell you filled in the spaces with handwritin' like the scrawls made by ol' Cy."

Deacon Stebbins laughed shortly. "You forget I spent two years behin' bars for making a simple error in copying, an' I sure as hell don't intend to go into that cage again, friend."

108

"Don't forget I was in the next cell, an' I sure don't want to go there again. You had to sign Cy's signature, didn't you?"

"That I did. I had to sign an affidavit saying the will—the instrument—was made by me, Cy Blunt in this case."

"An' you forged Cy's name?"

"Perfect imitation, the clerk said."

"That clerk? He knows a hell of a lot, Deacon?"

Deacon Stebbins closed his eyes. His lips were compressed. Plainly he fought pain. His fingers stroked his violin's polished back. Finally his thin lids opened.

"He got paid. And paid plenty."

Brennan nodded slowly. "But when a man has a gun under his brisket an' the hammer's eared back an' that hammer can fall an' blast the man into Kingdom Come—This Luke Kimlock. He overlooks no bets, Deacon."

"I've been thinkin' the same . . ."

"I could send Neefy to Beaverton. He could tend to it in some alley—from ambush—"

"Send him tomorrow."

Brennan said, "Better. Much better. Goodnight, friend."

"Goodnight, Silver."

Brennan descended the stairs. The guard squatted in shadows, gun pulled around so his hand rested on its butt. The guard said nothing. Neefy awaited where the alley ended.

"He's got a hen on," Neefy said.

They swung into step. "He'll get over it," Brennan said.

They went toward Brennan's saloon. They were on the long porch when the gun boomed above the bank.

They stopped, listening.

There were no independent sounds. The shooting was one blur of continuous roaring. Then, firing stopped.

"Re-loadin'," Neefy said. "He'll shoot again. He never shoots less than twice. Never."

Within minutes the six-shooter again snarled, leaped, spat death. Again, no single sounds—just one accumulated roar.

Then, silence.

Soon the lamplight left the bank's windows. "He's turnin' in," Neefy said. "He sleeps in his chair mostly, now—too much trouble to git into bed."

"He's fast," Brennan said.

"He's more than fast. He's chained lightnin'."

They crossed the porch to the brightly lighted saloon. From inside over the batwing doors came the sounds of drunkedness, a harpy's shrill feigned laugh.

"I doubt if there's a faster gun in Montana Territory," Brennan said.

"You're coverin' a wide area, Silver," Neefy said. "I need a drink. '

"Me, too," Brennan said.

8

STIRRUP RIVER ran through a deep cut a hundred feet north of Circle Diamond's ranch house. To keep flood water from undermining the south bank, Brennan and Stebbins had riprapped the bank with stone.

They'd also built a basement under their big stone house. Two days later Luke Kimlock, naked to the waist, crept into the basement out of the tunnel Quarter Circle V was digging between the house and the river.

Luke studied the pile of loose dirt on the basement's floor. "Lots of dirt there, Wobbly Head. Dang it, we must be close to the river, brother."

"Let's measure, brother."

Wobbly Head picked up a spotcord rope. He crawled into the tunnel and disappeared.

The rope moved in behind him. Finally, the rope stopped moving. "I'm at the far end, brother." His voice was distant and weak.

"Hang on tight," Luke said, picking up the rope.

He pulled it taut, marking the spot with a wire he tied around the rope. "Okay, brother."

The rope went slack. Luke Kimlock pulled it out, Wobbly Head creeping out behind the rope. They'd measured a yard on the basement floor and they measured the length of rope against this.

"How much more diggin'?" Wobbly Head asked.

"Not too much," Luke said. "A few more hours ought to see us hittin' the stone riprap."

"Hope so. I'm tired of workin' in the dark."

Wobbly Head climbed back into the tunnel, dragging a bucket behind him, a rope tied to the bucket's bail. An oldster came down the concrete stairway from the kitchen. He carried a lighted kerosene lantern that cast shadows on the stone walls.

"Cy wants to talk to you, Luke."

Luke stabbed a glance at Hank Chapman, Quarter Circle V's elderly foreman. "His wound gettin' worse, Hank?"

"No, I think not. Swollen a lot, though. That doc didn't do no good. Cy seems to have somethin' on his mind."

"You take over here?"

"Gladly. Who's in the hole?"

113

"Wobbly Head."

"Good place for him. Then he can't get into any mischief." The rope suddenly jerked two times. "Signalin' for me to pull out the bucket, I reckon." And Hank Chapman's rope scarred hands took hold of the spotcord. "Let 'er come, Wobbly Head."

Luke Kimlock went upstairs. Quarter Circle V guards squatted beside windows, rifles at the ready. Now and then a Circle Diamond bullet whammed into one of the rooms. All window panes had been broken.

Uncle Cy was in a bedroom, a blanket pulled over the window. Luke Kimlock had to accustom his eyes to the semi-darkness. "How's the wound, Unc?"

"Damn sore, nephew. But that ain't why I sent for you. I'm ashamed of myself, I am. I've held back somethin' on you."

Luke squatted on his bootheels, back to the wall. "You aren't the first one," he said. "A few females I've known have done the same."

"My will, Luke."

"What about your will?"

"It was robbed from me. The day them bastards ambushed me."

114

Luke nodded. "Why haven't you told me before?"

"Ashamed of myself. Foolish ol' man, ridin' right into an ambush—an' I should have rid the ridges, knowin' them two was out after me. But you know this bullet hole might kill me, so I'd best confess."

Luke Kimlock waited.

"Well, I was ridin' that day to Beaverton for one purpose, an' one only—to file a will I'd hand-writ leavin' all my earthly possessions to you, my only livin' kin."

"Let's not get melodramatic," Luke said.

Uncle Cy bristled. "Fer God's sake, dang your buttons, Luke, do you wanna hear the rest, or not?"

"As long as there's money involved, I'm interested. Go on, Cy."

"Well, that bullet knocks me from my hoss about halfway between Quarter Circle V an' Stirrup City. I'm sittin' there on my bottom, dazed, an' then the sun goes out, 'cause I reckon somebody come in behin' an' poleaxed me senseless."

"You've told me that before."

"But I ain't tol' you about the will. I somehow manage to roll into the brush—to this

115

day, things ain't clear, an' they look for me but they cain't fin' me."

"You've told me that before, too."

"Oh, yeah, my will. Well, it was gone. Somebody robbed me of it. An' the more I think of it, I'm sure that somebody workin' for me—somebody what knew about the will—tol' Brennan an' Stebbins about it, so they decided to get it then an' now."

Luke Kimlock was silent for a while. This put a new light on the entire set up. "I still can't see how you kept from seein' at least one of them, if there was more than one—what with them—or him—trompin' around in the brush lookin' for you."

"I fainted from lack of blood, like I told you. I was lucky they didn't fin' me an' shoot my brains out."

"If you have any of those," Luke Kimlock said. "Who'd be on your ranch knowing about you totin' this will?"

"Could have been a number of my hands."

Luke nodded. "That puts that out. You know what I think?"

"What?" Guardedly.

"I think you got a hunch that bullet wound will kill you. You intended to keep this secret.

116

You some day hoped to meet the fink that ambushed you an' kill him yourself. I think you know who he was."

"Honest Injun I don't, nephew. I jus' got thinkin' that if a man went to the clerk an' recorder in Beaverton, he might fin' out who filed that will 'cause the will has been changed. You're not my heir now. Silver Brennan an' Deacon Stebbins are."

"You've told me that, too. Have you seen the recording of the will?"

"Have I? Hell, yes. Damn young whipper-snapper of a clerk in the county office took it out for me to see. Had the county sheriff with him when they took possession of Quarter Circle V!"

"He had the original will?"

"He sure did have. Said he'd keep it a week longer. Law read that way, he said. I grabbed for it but the sheriff grabbed my han' an' I couldn't get it an tear it up."

Luke shifted positions. Stones were hot against his back for this room was on the south side, facing the hot sun.

"Let's get somethin' straight, Unc. Where my name had been hand-written into the will, there was the name of Deacon Stebbins or

117

Silver Brennan. What did you write in, ink or pencil?"

"Didn't have a pen aroun'. Had ink, though. Couldn't fin' a pen on the ranch, so I writ it in pencil."

Luke rose. "And pencil can be erased. How did the writing of the names of Brennan an' Stebbins look to you?"

"Jus' like they'd originally been writ in, Luke."

Luke said, "We need that will. Wonder where it is now?"

"Should be in Beaverton at the clerk's office in the court-house."

"Somebody's coming," Luke said.

Wobbly Head burst into the room, covered with dirt. "By damn, Luke, we reached them river rocks! I got one with my pick. He rolled down into the river. You can see daylight, Luke!"

"Hope no Circle Diamond hand heard the rock roll," Luke said.

"Nobody did. I stuck my head out. I looked aroun', I did. All they was was my head, the rocks lined up, an' the river."

"Well, we got a clear way out," Luke said.

"An' hosses t'other side of the river,"

Wobbly Head said, "an' our saddles an' tack there. Where we goin', brother?"

"I don't know where you're goin'," Luke said, "but I do know I'm riding into Beaverton."

"Cain't I go, brother?" Anxiously.

Luke looked at Cy Blunt. "You pay his wages, Unc. Makes no never-mind to me if he comes or stays."

Wobbly Head turned on Uncle Cy. "Uncle, please let me go with Luke!" His voice was pleading.

Uncle Cy winced. "My danged shoulder. That quack never did me a bit of good. Yeah, you can go. Git outa my sight, both of you."

Ten minutes later Luke Kimlock and Wobbly Head were in the timber on Stirrup River's gentle northern bank, emptying their boots of Stirrup River water. Because of the drought, the river was low and water had come only to their knees.

Their boots emptied, they legged through the timber, each carrying a loaded Winchester .30–30 rifle, each moving as silently as possible. Overhead the hot noon sun hammered down.

They came to the mouth of a low coulee.

119

Here the timber petered out. "You take that ridge, I take this," Luke told Wobbly Head.

"Okay, brother."

Boulders and sandstones cluttered up the ridges. Luke moved from one to the other, the terrain clearly seen below. Back of him was Stirrup River, flowing lazily through cottonwoods and boxelders; beyond the river the stone buildings of Circle Diamond.

He looked about for landmarks. By now he should be opposite the hiding-place of the horses. He looked west into the coulee below. He saw no horses or horsetender.

Fear struck him. Had Stebbins and Brennan men discovered the hiding-place and hit? He went downward, moving from boulder to boulder, rifle in hand, boots carefully placed so he'd not slip in shale or dislodge a rock to warn anybody below of his coming.

He met Wobbly Head in a cottonwood grove. "Where's Edwin?" Wobbly Head asked. "An' our cayuses?"

"Right here."

The voice came from behind. Both whirled, rifles rising. The rifles steadied, then lowered. Luke Kimlock said, "Don't ever do that again, man. I almost emptied my .30–30 into you."

"Jes' playin' a trick, Luke," Edwin said.

Luke shook his head. "Man, no tricks are permissible in this war. This is dog eat dog, an' I don't want to be the dog eaten."

"Your cayuses are hidden against the far bank," Edwin said.

They went north through buckbrush. Luke's buckskin nickered softly upon seeing his master. Wobbly Head drew back, staring at the ground. "That's—that's blood there, ain't it?"

"That sure is," Edwin said, "an' over yonder lays the fink what shed it, men."

Luke Kimlock had already spotted the body. The dead man lay in the shadow of a sandstone boulder. He'd already begun to bloat. His belly protruded around his pant's belt.

A rifle lay beside the corpse. Beside the rifle lay a filled cartridge-belt whose holster held a pistol, undoubtedly a .45.

Wobbly Head stared down. "That's Brent Torgot," he said. "He works for Stebbins an' Brennan."

"He DID work for them," Edwin stated. "Right now he's got a shovel heavin' in coal."

Wobbly Head looked at Edwin. "Explain?"

Luke Kimlock listened while he saddled his buckskin. "He come sneakin' in about four hours ago. I come in behin' him. I asked him what he was doin' here," Edwin related.

"Yeah?" Wobbly Head said.

"He turned quick. He fired one with his rifle, but I shot for sure an' he shot by heck. The for sure guy won."

"Sure looks like it," Wobbly Head said.

"What'll I do with him?" Edwin asked.

Both men looked at Luke Kimlock, now tightening his tackaberry buckle. "Tie him across his horse," Luke said, "an' lead the bronc to the edge of town after dark, an' then let the horse take the corpse down mainstreet. Somewhere aroun' Brennan's saloon somebody will see what's happenin', an' Brennan can have the honor of untying him from saddle."

Edwin said, "Say, that's a good idea. An' besides it'll show Brennan an' Stebbins they're in a real war."

"Saddle your horse," Luke told Wobbly Head. "We can't stay here all day lookin' at a dead man."

Soon Luke Kimlock and Wobbly Head rode north. They rode up coulee a mile, then reined in, hidden by brush. Luke slipped from saddle, field-glasses in hand, and moved into the clear, where he studied their backtrail from behind a boulder.

No riders trailed.

The two then rode east, traveling high country. Within a few miles, Luke Kimlock said, "Wobbly Head, we got to split up. You ride to the north, me to the south. Keep high. Watch the ground below. Don't skyline yourself unless you can't avoid it."

"Best, brother."

"From what Uncle Cy says, we come first to the railroad construction camp, about twenty miles down-river east. Then some twenty miles beyond the camp we ride into Beaverton."

"He tol' you correct, brother."

Luke glanced at the youth's wide, ugly face. "Somethin' bothering you, boy?"

"Life's kinda funny in lots of ways, ain't it now? Brent Torgot tries to sneak up on Edwin but Edwin sneaks up on Brent Torgot instead."

"What's so odd about that?"

"Not that, so much—but Brent shoots first an' Ed shoots second. By rights, Brent should've killed Edwin, not the other aroun'."

Luke Kimlock studied the youth. Sometimes

Wobbly Head didn't seem so mentally lacking as he was supposed to be.

"The answer is simple," Luke said.

"What is the answer, brother?"

"Sometimes the guy who takes aim an' shoots second wins," Luke Kimlock said. "Come on, climb that ridge."

Wobbly Head neckreined his bay around, hit him with his Garcia spurs, and loped up a slope, bronc kicking stones and gravel. Luke Kimlock sat his prancing buckskin and watched.

The boy hit the ridge, lifted his hand, then disappeared behind the rimrock. Luke Kimlock nodded. The boy learned rapidly. Luke touched his buckskin with his Amarillo spurs.

The buckskin loped east.

9

EVENING of that same day found Deacon Stebbins alone in his upstairs quarters softly playing his violin, bow moving slowly. Hurrying boots sounded outside on the stairway.

Scowling, he lowered his violin, mood broken. He recognized two sets of boots. Knuckles pounded on the door.

"Who is it?"

The guard said, "The swamper from Mr. Brennan's saloon, Mr. Stebbins."

'What does he want?"

"He wants to talk to you. He says it's very important. He bears no arms. I searched him, as you ordered me to do to everybody who comes in but Mr. Brennan."

"I don't want to see him."

"He says it's very important."

"All right. Let him in."

The guard's key sounded in the lock. The door opened. Lamplight showed the swamper's whiskery face. "Silver Brennan sent me over,

Mr. Stebbins. Brent Torgot just got into town."

"Who's Brent Torgot?"

"He works for your Circle Diamon'. He come in doubled over his saddle, hands tied to the cinch-rings, his boots the same on the other side."

Deacon Stebbins said impatiently, "Continue, fella. Get it off your mind. Was Torgot drunk?"

"Not a drop of booze in him, I'd say. Me an' Mr. Brennan an' the others went out right away. Brent Torgot had been shot. He's plumb dead, Mr. Stebbins."

"That all you got to say, old man?"

"Ain't it enough?"

"Throw him out," Deacon Stebbins told the guard.

The guard said, "He'd break every bone slidin' down the stairs."

"Throw him out."

The guard grabbed for the swamper. The old man was too quick. He ran wildly down-stairs, cursing Deacon Stebbins, who sat in his chair and grinned, idly caressing his violin.

He had the violin to his chin when Silver Brennan entered, the guard behind him.

Brennan stood in the doorway and waited until the banker had finished. The music, wild, tempestuous, filled the room, echoing from the walls.

Deacon Stebbins sat there in the dim light, his shadow moving against the wall. Brennan listened stony faced. Finally the bow paused, the last note died.

"Well," Deacon Stebbins asked.

"Nobody seems to know where the horse come from, an' nobody seems to know who killed him."

"Quarter Circle V killed him," Deacon Stebbins said. "Naturally, that's so. And it makes little matter where he was killed."

Silver Brennan had no words.

"The point is that he's dead," Deacon Stebbins said. "He didn't matter. He never was much. But what matters is that Quarter Circle V won some more points—lots of points, Brennan."

The guard listened. Silver Brennan said, "In what way, Deacon?"

"The town. The damned whole town. When you lose, and we lost here—well, the people start slipping away."

"That's true," Brennan said.

Deacon Stebbins said, "An' I'm tied down. I can't get on a horse. I can't ride out an' get revenge." He looked down at his violin, lying in his lap.

Finally the banker raised his head.

Brennan said, "You've got a rifle. It knocked down O'Rourke. Why can't it send this Kimlock bastard from saddle?"

Stebbins studied the saloon-keeper. "What the hell do you use for brains? Sawdust?"

Brennan hid anger. His future in Stirrup City depended upon this banker, for if Stebbins fell he also fell—for if Stebbins lost his hold on Stirrup City, townspeople would demand he and his saloon and prostitutes would go.

And if they didn't leave, the townspeople would drive them out.

"No insults, please," Brennan said, "but I don't follow you, Deacon."

"I drop him from his horse—like I did O'Rourke—and this town blows up in our faces, Silver. This Luke Kimlock is no bum, no gun bum, like O'Rourke. When I killed O'Rourke, I did Stirrup City a favor, but if I murdered Kimlock in cold blood—No, Silver, no."

"I see your point," Brennan said.

128

"Where's Kimlock now?"

"Our man just rid in from the railroad camp. Said Kimlock an' thet halfwit came into the camp about five this afternoon."

Deacon Stebbins' brows rose. "Anybody see him leave the ranch?"

Silver Brennan shook his head. "All claim he never left the ranch, Deacon. Or, if he did, they never seen him. The boys guardin' out there jes' can't understand how he got through them."

"Who's the halfwit?"

"Thet punk ridin' for ol' Cy. The one they call Wobbly Head."

Deacon Stebbins thought and then said, "I got him placed now. Heavy-set, wide face, ugly as sin, supposed to be half-loco."

"What do you reckon Kimlock aims to do at the camp, Deacon?" Silver Brennan asked.

Deacon Stebbins laughed shortly. "Do I have to draw you a picture? He'll talk right-of-way with the boss."

"He won't get nowhere there. We got all right-of-way tied up from two miles this side of the camp to beyon' Quarter Circle V five miles up river, an' we'll get our price 'cause it'll be cheaper to meet our price than build expensive right-of-way aroun' through them rough hills."

Stebbins spoke to the guard. "Go down to your post. Our conversation doesn't include you."

The guard left.

Stebbins said, "Then he'll ask to see some hides of cattle the camp has recently butchered. He'll inspect brands to make sure we haven't been sellin' the camp his uncle's Quarter Circle V beef."

"All hides he'll find will have our Circle Diamon' on them," Brennan said. "What'd we do next?"

"What would you do?"

"I'd kill Kimlock. With him gone, ol' Cy is almost helpless, shot up like he is."

"How about ol' Cy Blunt's crew?"

Brennan shook his head. "Cowhands aren't like the way Western stories read—ready to fight to the death for their boss and their iron. That's bull put out by them Hudson River boys. With Kimlock dead, with ol' Cy completely out of commission—or dead, too— then Quarter Circle V men will throw up hands an' get out with their hides, if they can."

"You know cowpunchers," Stebbins complimented.

"I should. I've had enough experience with them."

"All right, kill Kimlock. Order Neefy to trail him to the camp, then kill him—kill him anyway Neefy wants, jus' so Kimlock's dead, Brennan."

"I'll get Neefy movin'." Silver Brennan left. Deacon Stebbins picked up his violin. He played gently, softly. Outside citizens paused, listened. Mrs. Rothwell said to Mrs. Hannigan, "He plays happy. I guess he's finally got Luke Kimlock killed."

"I hope not," Mrs. Hannigan said.

"Jack was in the saloon for his usual afternoon brew," Mrs. Rothwell said, "an' he heard Kimlock's out at the railroad camp, very much alive."

"Only takes a second to kill a man," Mrs. Hannigan said.

Silver Brennan returned to his bar. A bunch of railroad hands were in town celebrating. They were half drunk and noisy, the din rolling out into Stirrup City's main street.

Neefy was not around. A bartender told him Neefy was upstairs with a new girl named Molly.

Brennan climbed the stairs. His madame—a

131

fat woman—sat behind her desk. To get to her crib a girl had to pass the desk. She confirmed the bartender's statement.

"You want him, boss?"

"Tell him to meet me down below."

"I'll get him."

Brennan stood with his back to the bar watching one of his blackjack dealers in operation. "I was bedded down for the night," Neefy grumbled.

Brennan relayed Deacon Stebbins' orders. Neefy scowled and said he didn't like night riding. "But you like the hundred bucks a week you get from me an' Brennan, don't you?"

Neefy grinned. "I love it. I'm on my way. Luke Kimlock is as good as dead, boss."

Brennan merely nodded.

Neefy started away. Brennan caught his arm. "Jes' a minute. You know this Mike Hanna fella?"

"The dude down in Beaverton, workin' in the court house?"

"That's the man. You kill him, too."

Neefy scowled. "Why?"

"My business, not yours. You ride directly to Beaverton. You kill Hanna. Then when

Kimlock rides in, you kill him. Or kill him where you get a chance—in town, out of town."

"They're both as good as dead."

"Now, the price."

"My usual price. Two hundred bucks a head." Brennan laughed sardonically. "You never drew down two hundred bucks a head in your life, an' you know it. One hundred a head."

Neefy shook his head. "Hanna is nothin', but Kimlock—he's a hoss of a different color, Brennan. He's a gunman, not a courthouse sissy."

They dickered. They settled at one-fifty a head. Neefy started toward the stairway. Again, Brennan caught his arm.

"If anythin' goes wrong, Neefy, jus' forget you ever heard of Silver Brennan an' Deacon Stebbins, savvy."

Neefy laughed. "Nothin' will go wrong." He tapped his holster significantly. "I'll throw a few things together an' leave right away, but I want half down now, an' in gold."

"Fair enough."

Brennan went behind the bar to a cash box. He paid in eagles. Neefy pocketed the money and said, "When I ride past I'll give the ol'

133

rebel yell." He was rather drunk, Brennan realized.

"Better sober up, friend," the saloon keeper advised.

"I'm sober now."

Neefy went upstairs. Brennan moved closer to the blackjack dealer. He smiled faintly. Every drunk said he was sober and he could be staggering and slurring his words when he said same.

He turned his attention to the blackjack dealer. The last few nights this particular blackjack table had been showing less than its fifty percent profit. The dealer was new. This was his fourth night on the job.

Brennan knew his business. He considered all men dishonest because he himself was dishonest. He knew he was in a dishonest business. Therefore the business would be transacted by dishonest men.

Two things could be wrong at this table. One, the dealer could be knocking down on the house. Two, the dealer might not know blackjack.

Brennan soon discovered the dealer was inept. He had a ten spot up and he hit himself.

Brennan almost shivered despite the night's heat. This man knew nothing about blackjack.

He couldn't bluff.

He was also inept in his knocking-down. Brennan saw him openly pocket house money.

"I'll send a man to relieve you," he told the dealer. "Then please come to my office, Mister Silbermann."

"Something wrong?"

"Not a thing. Jus' a friendly talk."

"I'll be right in."

Brennan returned to the bar. He spoke over his shoulder to a bartender. "Send Joe to take over Table Two, Ike."

Soon Joe slid in. The new man slid out. Brennan caught the eye of his roughest bouncer —a big, red-headed Irishman. He nodded toward his office. The bouncer went that direction.

Brennan caught the eye of another tough bouncer. Again, the same nod. The bouncer went toward the office, a cubicle set in the corner at the saloon's southern end.

The first bouncer entered ahead of the black-jack dealer, the second bouncer behind him. Brennan began a slow walk toward his closed office door. At that moment, Neefy loped by.

Neefy threw up his head. From his throat broke the old rebel Confederate yell. Stirrup City's rafters vibrated.

Neefy rode his top bronc, a blazed-faced, white-stockinged bay. He raised his .45 high. Five shots were blasted into the sky.

Then, another yell.

And the bay had disappeared around the corner. Brennan continued on toward his office. One of his newest girls, wearing far less than the law allowed, had her small hands over her ears.

"Has he gone?"

Brennan nodded.

The hands came down. The girl smiled her frozen harpy smile at her boss. "Jus' like Texas," she giggled.

"I wouldn't know," Silver Brennan said. "I've never been in Texas, baby."

He continued toward his office.

10

THE railroad's dirt boss told Luke Kimlock that he and Wobbly Head could sleep that night in a railroad tent. Luke Kimlock turned him down. "Too easy to sneak in for an ambush, but thanks."

"Ambush?"

"Yes, ambush."

Luke Kimlock and Wobbly Head spent the night in the brush along Stirrup River, their camping-grounds circled by catchropes tied a foot above the ground.

"Anybody try to sneak in an' the rope'll trip 'em," Wobbly Head said. "Good idea Where'd you learn that, brother?"

"Old ranger trick. Which shift you want— from now to midnight or midnight to dawn?"

"Which do you crave?"

"Either one's okay with me."

"I'll sit guard until midnight."

Kimlock said, "I don't like to call you Wobbly Head. What's your real name?"

"Only got one. No second name, no last

name. I dunno who was my pa or ma. Uncle Cy picked me up in Omaha. He'd shipped some stock there. I was about four, he tol' me."

Kimlock nodded.

"Said nobody claimed me, so he did. But I did know my first name was Elmer."

Luke Kimlock hit the ground. He was immediately asleep. When Wobbly Head shook him awake he sat up and noticed the moon was gone and stars alone shimmered overhead.

"It's past midnight. Why didn't you wake me sooner?"

"You're Uncle Cy's nephew."

"What's that got to do with it?"

"I didn't finish my story last night. When Uncle Cy found me he was bummin' aroun' buyin' cattle. He couldn't keep me with him so he put me in a school in Omaha."

Luke Kimlock pulled on a boot.

"Then Uncle Cy got hold of Quarter Circle V. So he had a place for me. An' he took me out to Montana."

"I understand."

"I'd die for Uncle Cy."

"I hope you don't have to," Luke said. "Anything happen in the night?"

"On the wagon road. Neefy rode east."

The wagon-trail was about a hundred yards south. Luke pulled on another boot. "Not too much moon last night. Quite a piece to the road. How could you tell?"

"By his horse. Bay, with a blazed face an' two white stockings, both front legs. I know every horse in Stirrup Basin be it a Quarter Circle V or a Circle Diamon' mount."

Luke Kimlock got to his feet. He looked south at the railroad right-of-way camp. Brown, dirty tents, stretching out, with no lights. Lights in the long tent—the mess-hall, though.

There cooks and flunkies were getting breakfast ready for the hundreds of dirty men who soon would be moving prairie sod with mules and horses pulling slips or frenos.

"He stop at the camp?"

"No he rode right on, brother. Headin' for Beaverton."

"What time was that?"

"Moon said about ten thirty, closer to eleven. But a man can't tell time good by the moon like he can from the sun."

Luke Kimlock scowled. "Let's go eat, Wobbly Head."

"I thought you was goin' call me Elmer, brother."

Kimlock smiled. "Wobbly Head is better."

"I agree."

The head cook grudgingly fed them. "I ain't runnin' a restraw," he grumbled. "This is for dirt men, only."

Kimlock picked up a tin plate and tools. He moved from kettle to kettle, selecting what he wanted, Wobbly Head following suit, the burly cook glaring at them, eyes small and mean.

Kimlock had what he wanted. He patted the cook on the shoulder. "The hell you say. I thought this was a public cafe."

The cook wisely remained silent.

The Quarter Circle V men were the cook's first customers. Soon dirt men drifted in. Camp orders made them wash first outside. Here were tubs of water and wash basins and soap and roller towels.

The men splashed and gurgled and bellyached. By then Quarter Circle V had finished eating. Kimlock and Wobbly Head dumped their dirty plates and tools in the tub of water and went out.

"We forgot to thank the cook." Wobbly Head showed a wide grin.

"Good lord, how thoughtless." Kimlock stood and looked about, picking his teeth.

He was tall, rugged, tough gun tied down. "Wonder where the slaughter area is?"

"Down along the river in the timber. I was there once about two weeks ago with Uncle Cy."

Kimlock belched.

"They butcher a beef or two a day. They throw the guts into the river. That's why they butcher in the timber."

"They throw hides in the river, too?"

"I dunno. No hides was aroun' when me an' Unc was here, an' he came to look at brands."

"They might have known he was comin'."

"Unc figgered that, an' he tol' the head butcher what he figgered. For a while, I thought they'd go for their irons, brother."

"The butcher packed a side-arm?"

"He sure did."

Luke Kimlock said, "That seems odd. He must've been expectin' trouble. A pistol on your hip'd be only in your way when you butchered. I got a hunch we'll find no hides, Wobbly Head."

"We should've slept out in the bresh an' come in unexpectedly this mornin'."

Luke Kimlock shook his head. "Never would've worked, boy. Stebbins an' Brennan

141

know where you an' I are, all the time. Right now eyes somewhere are watchin' us."

"Neefy? Think he might set an ambush trap between here an' Beaverton?"

"Wouldn't put it beyond him," Luke Kimlock said. "Lead me to the slaughter grounds, boy."

"Down river in the bresh."

Luke Kimlock got what he had expected—nothing substantial. One beef hung on tripod, gutted and skinned and beheaded. The hide was not around. When he asked for it the head butcher said, "Damn cow never had no hide, cowboy. Wandered in here plumb naked."

"You're comical," Luke said.

The butcher was a big shouldered man of thirty odd. He had a gunbelt strapped around his middle, the holster holding a Smith and Wesson .38. Unbeseen by him, Wobbly Head had crept on hands and knees behind the man. The butcher's helpers watching, grinning slightly. None said a word.

"I can get funnier, cowboy!"

"I'll bet you can," Luke Kimlock said, and unexpectedly pushed the man backwards.

The man fell over Wobbly Head. He landed hard on his rump, pistol flying from leather.

His helpers broke out laughing. Wobbly Head got up, the gun in hand.

He handed the weapon to Luke Kimlock. Luke said, "He don't need this to skin a stolen beef." He threw the pistol into the river. It landed with a splash in shallow ripples.

Enraged, the butcher leaped to his feet, fists up. Luke Kimlock said, "Come on, buster," and the man came in, fists working. He never landed a blow. He went sailing over Luke Kimlock's head to land on his back, the jarring fall driving the wind out of him.

He rolled, clutching his back, gasping for air, all wind gone. His helpers stopped laughing. The swiftness of Luke Kimlock's move, the smoothness of it, astonished them.

Wobbly Head's mouth hung open. "How'd you—How'd you do that, brother?"

Luke Kimlock grinned. "Want me to show you how?" He made a playful grab for the youth, who darted out of reach. "Old ranger trick," Luke said. "Now let's go out an' look at the stock waitin' for the knife, huh?"

"This fink might want more trouble," the boy said.

Luke Kimlock looked at the butcher who

now sat up, clutching his lower backbone. "I believe he's out of commission for a while."

Luke and Wobbly Head rode down river to where a few head of fat steers grazed, awaiting their turns to be slaughtered. All wore the Stebbins—Brennan Circle Diamond brand.

"Six are new branded," Luke said thoughtfully. "They could have had Circle Diamon' run over Quarter Circle V, you know."

"Uncle Cy said a man could tell if a brand had been branded over," Wobbly Head said, "but I've forgot how."

"Not hard to prove. You skin the cow. You scrape the hide from inside, getting the fat off it—then you come to the brand. No matter how deep the new brand is burned, there's bound to be scar tissue showing the outlines of the old brand."

"That's why no hides are aroun' this butcherin', huh?"

"Could be."

"Shall we kill one of these steers? Cut out the branded part an' test it?"

Luke Kimlock shook his head. "We haven't got time, for one thing. Let's say they throw the hides in the river. There're beavers in this river, ain't there?"

"Yes, lots of them."

"Then there should be a beaver dam downstream somewhere," Luke said. "Come on, boy."

"I get it," Wobbly Head said. "The hides would work down stream to the dam, then get hung up there."

They encountered a beaver dam two miles down stream. It was a thick, high dam made of trees, mud and twigs. It held back quite a pool of water.

"Beavers live back in the bank," Wobbly Head said, "an' that's their holes to their dens back in the bank—those openin's level with the water."

"Lots of entrances so this must be a big colony, but there are no hides that I can see."

Wobbly Head pit his mount close to the water. "Look, brother!" He pointed down into the clearness. "There's a couple layin' on the bottom!"

The hides had become waterlogged. Wobbly Head took off his clothes, dived down, came up without hides. "Stuck in the mud, brother." He took a deep breath, then went down again.

This time he came up with a water soaked cowhide.

Luke Kimlock helped him pull the heavy hide onto the bank. "Get your clothes an' dress up on the bank," Luke ordered. "With your rifle."

"Afraid somebody might trail us?"

"Right. Shoot to hit if necessary."

Clothes in one hand, rifle in the other, the naked boy climbed up the cutbank while Luke Kimlock, sharp pocket-knife in hand, cut the brand out of the hide.

Evidently the cowhide had been in water some time for already it had shed its hair, leaving the hide a whitish slippery parchment, the outlines of the Circle Diamond brand clear on the outer side.

Suddenly Wobbly Head's rifle stuttered three times up on the cutbank. Luke Kimlock straightened, knife in one hand, piece of cowhide in the other, and hollered, "What goes on, boy?"

"Fink followin' us from the butcher camp, on foot. He ducked into the bresh back yonder. I salted the brush down."

"Did you hit him?"

"I don't know—" Again, the rifle spoke— two bullets, this time. Then a chuckle. "He come out runnin'. Headin' back toward the butcherin' area, an' dang fast."

"Let him go," Luke Kimlock said. "I cut out the brand. Let's make tracks for Beaverton."

Within a few minutes, they were high in the northern hills, the basin and wagon-road and the brush below them. They saw no sign of an ambush and when they rode into Beaverton Luke Kimlock laid the cut-out brand on the sheriff's desk.

"This might interest you, sheriff," he said.

11

NEEFY changed horses at Circle Diamond's Buggy Creek linecamp, peeling his kak off the blaze-faced bay and throwing it onto a tough blue roan gelding. Then, he pushed on again.

Dawn colored the east when he rode his lathered roan into Beaverton and stabled him in a small barn Circle Diamond had bought for Circle Diamond waddies. He turned his roan over to the old hostler, tugged his pistol into a higher position, and said, "How goes things?"

"Same as usual. How come you ride these forty miles from Stirrup City?"

Neefy said, "You ask too many damn questions, ol' man. What saloon is open?"

"All of them. They never close. Their owners ain't got no keys to their doors."

"You grow smarter as you grow older," Neefy sarcastically said. "You've been here 'longside the Stirrup City road all night?"

"Graveyard shift, Neefy."

"Ain't seen two riders come in from the

148

direction of Stirrup City? A boy about yeah high astraddle a Quarter Circle V cayuse an' a tall one about my age mounted on a lineback cream colored buckskin?"

"Ain't seen 'em. An' had they passed here, I'd not missed."

Neefy nodded. Luke Kimlock and the boy had undoubtedly spent the night back in the brush, maybe at the railroad camp. "Oats him an' hay him an' rub him down," Neefy said.

"Don't I do that to all of them?" Surlily.

Neefy drew back his right fist as if to hit the oldster. The hostler ducked, almost falling down. Neefy let his fist break. He said, "So much for you," and left.

Beaverton's two other livery barns were between him and the closest saloon, The Apple Barrel. Neefy checked in both. Luke Kimlock's buckskin was in neither. Kimlock had not yet ridden into the county seat.

Neefy realized that when Kimlock came into Beaverton he, Neefy, would have to go into hiding for were Kimlock to glimpse him Kimlock would naturally be suspicious.

He entered the Apple Barrel. The sawdust-floor smelled of stale beer and cigarette butts. Various drunks sat at various tables in various

149

states of drunkenness. Some slept on the floor or over tables. The morning bartenders had just donned aprons.

Neefy knew but one. The other two were new bartenders. He said, "A shot, Hellman," and then, "A little information, maybe?"

"Mabel?"

Neefy grinned. "How'd you guess?"

"A little bird tol' me. Upstairs in her room, I guess."

"Alone?"

"Dunno, friend. I jes' come on shift. She might be bedded down with an all nighter or not. Madame's at the head of the stairs. She'll know."

Neefy threw down his drink. He bought a bottle of Old Horseshoe. Bottle in hand, he climbed the wide stairs. The madame dozed on a couch. Mabel was alone.

Neefy started down the hall. The madame's stern voice halted him. "I know you're her friend, but even friends pay in this joint, cowboy."

Neefy tossed her a quarter eagle. She caught it, sunk an eyetooth into it, then nodded. "Go on, cowboy."

Neefy smiled tightly. "Thanks, bitch."

She glared at him. He stopped before door seventeen. He hadn't been in town for some time. Did Mabel have Crib seventeen or sixteen?

"Sweet seventeen," the madame called.

"Thanks."

The third session of hard knocking brought Mabel to the door. She peered out, clutching her robe. "What the hell do you want, cowboy?"

"You don't remember me?"

"Wait'll I get my eyes in focus. Oh, yes, you're Watson?"

"Watson, hell," Neefy said. "Do I come in or don't I?"

The madame listened carefully, synthetic redhead cocked. Neefy grinned. Were Mabel to turn him down, the madame would turn Mabel out. Neefy knew he had the woman over a barrel.

The prostitute looked down the hall, saw the madame and immediately said, "Come on in, Mr. Matthews."

Neefy slid inside. The door closed behind him. Mabel locked it. She slipped out of her robe and stood naked. "You paid the madame?"

"Two bucks an' a half."

"I'm sleepy. Bunch of railroad boys were in last night. None of us girls got any sleep. You can't have much time."

"I won't need much," Neefy said.

Ten minutes later, he was in the hall again. The madame had a spare room at the end of the hall. She was short of girls, thus the vacancy. Yes, he could rent it at a buck a day.

"Should I send in a girl later on?"

Neefy said, "I'll let you know."

"Would you like me to visit you? I'll be off shift soon an' I'll be just' as good in your bed as in mine alone."

"How much?"

"Half eagle. For all day, too."

Neefy was bone-tired. Night before last he'd drunk all night in Brennan's saloon. He'd spent last night in a saddle. He did some thinking. He reasoned he had time. By rights Kimlock shouldn't ride into Beaverton until about noon.

"Okay, but I have to get up at aroun' ten."

"You'll get little sleep with me, cowboy."

Neefy was in the county court house at eleven. He had seen Mike Hanna but once, and then at a distance and he wanted to be sure he killed the right man.

Hanna was chunky, short, blonde and in his middle twenties, Neefy guessed. "You Mr. Hanna?" Neefy asked.

"I am. What can I do for you?"

"I'm a hired hand of Mr. Brennan, back in Stirrup City. He sent me to town to check on a homestead entry. The name is Joseph Borowsky, Mr. Hanna."

Hanna repeated the name slowly, thinking, and then, "I can remember no homestead entry filed in such a name. Here's my deed book. Take it to a table and look it over."

"I might have the name wrong," Neefy said.

Neefy carried the ledger to a table. From here he studied Mike Hanna under heavy brows.

His right hand went into his Levi pocket. His fingers fondled the strychnine pill there. Doc Miller had given him the pill before he'd left Stirrup City.

He'd complained about a coyote howling all night outside his window on Circle Diamond. "Put this pill in a hunk of meat and he'll howl no more," the doctor had said.

Neefy intended to feed the pill to Mike Hanna, not a coyote. When the courthouse closed for dinner he trailed Mike Hanna to the Shoe Box, a beanery on the main street.

Another courthouse worker, a bony, middle-aged man, accompanied Mike Hanna.

The Shoe Box had no empty seats so the two men went on to the Apple Barrel Saloon, Neefy hearing Mike Hanna say that at the Apple Barrel a man could eat free with the purchase of a bottle of beer and that the Apple Barrel was serving roast beef today.

Neefy scowled. The presence of the middle-aged man balled things up. He figured somehow he'd get the strychnine into Mike Hanna's grub but with the other man along . . . would he have to poison both to get at Hanna?

Hanna and his companion entered the Apple Barrel. Neefy went around through the alley to the saloon's rear door. He looked through the kitchen window.

A hairy armed heavy set man was the cook. The waitress was a saloon prostitute. Neefy heard her say, "Mike Hanna and Vincent Smith from the court-house, cook. Both are important men. A thicker slice of beef for both, huh?"

"Okay, Jennie."

The cook cut two exceptionally thick slices from the roast, putting each on a tin plate. "That should fill 'em up," he grumbled. "There's your other order, girl. I need a loaf of bread. No, I'll get it. You got orders to deliver."

"Good boy, Mark."

The waitress picked up three tin plates laden with beef and spuds and hurried into the saloon, disappearing. The cook waddled into his pantry. Neefy acted quickly.

He darted into the kitchen. He pulled shut the pantry door and slid the bolt in, locking in the cook, who immediately began kicking the door and hollering to be let out.

Within seconds, the pill, now in two parts, rested deep in the two slices of roast destined for Hanna and his friend and Neefy was outside circling around to enter the saloon from the front.

The waitress came in with Hanna's order. "Danged cook's mad," Neefy heard her say. "Bolt accident'ly slid shut while he was in the kitchen. An' he blames me, of course."

"Always a problem," Mike Hanna joked.

Neefy stood at the bar. He studied the two slabs of beef resting before the two county workers. A sudden fear hit him. Those slabs looked thinner than the ones he'd doctored.

Hanna and his friend began eating. Mug of beer before him, Neefy watched them in the backbar mirror. The two ate rapidly. The roasts disappeared and nothing happened.

Neefy scowled. Something was wrong here. Doc Miller had said the pill would kill a coyote in his tracks. And here these two had eaten the roasts and nothing . . .

Suddenly, a man down-bar screamed.

Neefy's head jerked around. The man had risen to his feet at his table. He suddenly fell to lie inert.

His companion started up, clutched his throat. His eyes bugged out. Then he too, fell.

Neefy put his head in his hands. His fingers trembled. The waitress had served Mike Hanna and his friend the wrong slabs of roast.

Neefy had killed two innocent men.

"Holy smoke," Neefy said.

The waitress ran out calling, "Doctor, doctor! Somebody get a doctor, quick!"

Neefy lifted his mug. His hands were steady now. Reason came in—all men had to die and what difference did it make to the world if a man died right now or later on?

Further reasoning came in: the two had died sudden, painless deaths. Much better than lingering around with something slowly eating you from inside. The backbar showed a tall man with the proverbial doctor's valise entering. The man knelt beside the dead men. "No, I can't tell you what killed them until I have an autopsy on them," the doctor told the worried cook.

Neefy left his beer unfinished and walked outside to sit on a bench on the long porch.

Two women, plainly housewives, came hurrying toward the saloon. One carried a baby and had a young boy and girl following her. The other was big with child and had a small boy behind her.

The women were weeping. The two families entered the saloon. Soon the fat sheriff waddled in, followed by a lanky deputy.

Neefy scowled.

All was a babble inside the saloon. Neefy got to his feet. He went into the alley and north to the back door of the livery stable. With the sheriff and deputy occupied, now was a good time to act.

He'd seen the old hostler enter the saloon; therefore, the barn should hold only animals, no humans. His assumption was correct. He looked carefully about, saw nobody and then went to the saddles.

All saddles except one had rifles in scabbards,

stocks sticking upward. Some had the names of their owners engraved on their steel butt plates. He picked a .30–30 with the name CARL SEEGER engraved.

Kneeling, he kicked the cartridge out of the barrel, caught it in midair, saw a fresh shell slip into the chamber. He then pushed the ejected shell into the magazine and straightened.

Neefy grinned. He didn't know Carl Seeger but Seeger would be in for a surprise when the sheriff tapped him on the shoulder, Seeger's Winchester rifle in hand.

Again, he carefully looked about but saw only the rumps of horses, the row of saddles, the bridles and hackamores hanging on the wall. He breathed deeply and, rifle in hand, returned to the alley.

A few minutes later Mike Hanna hurried toward the court-house. He was almost running. He was ten minutes late. His boss was a stickler for promptness.

He was alone on the street, for the rest of Beaverton crowded around the corpses in the saloon.

Neefy knelt hidden in the small space between the Mercantile and the Express. He'd never before shot this rifle. Did it shoot true?

It shot true.

The bullet tore off the top of Mike Hanna's head.

A few minutes later, the sheriff found the rifle lying between the buildings where Neefy had purposely dropped it. Soon a protesting and half-drunk Carl Seeger was in handcuffs and being dragged toward the jail.

Neefy watched from the saloon's porch. Only one more remained.

Ride into town, Luke Kimlock!

12

SEEMINGLY bored, the fat sheriff studied the cowhide, then raised slow and insolent pale blue eyes to look at tall Luke Kimlock. This task completed, he then glanced at Wobbly Head who apparently did not interest him for his eyes moved back on Kimlock.

"So you're Cy Blunt's nephew, huh? Heard thet since you rid into Stirrup City's there been nothin' but trouble. That right?"

His authoritative tone rankled Luke Kimlock. "All depends on your point-of-view," Kimlock said. "Now this cowhide, sheriff."

"What about it?"

"Its original brand was Quarter Circle V. Somebody's branded a Circle Diamond over it."

"I can read brands, son. I was born an' raised on a ranch. I fail to see what you're drivin' at."

"The original brand was my uncle's. Stebbins an' Brennan had their iron run over my uncle's. My uncle never sold Circle Diamon' a cow. That means Circle Diamon' stole this critter."

160

"Harsh words, Kimlock. From what I've heard, Brennan an' Stebbins now own Quarter Circle V. That'd give them the right to rebrand their own critters, in my book."

"This animal was rebranded many months ago. An' for the record, sheriff, my uncle never sold to Circle Diamon'."

The obese man shrugged heavy shoulders, still apparently bored by the proceedings. "None of my business, Kimlock, but I've done heard a will made by your uncle was filed in this court house an' it gives the good names of Stebbins an' Brennan as his heirs, denouncin' you."

"That will was stolen from my uncle's person when he was ambushed and evidently it was doctored—and besides, my uncle is still alive. You inherit from a dead man, not a live man."

"I know that, Kimlock, but the county court some days back declared your uncle mentally incompetent and therefore unable to take care of his own affairs properly."

"I've heard about that. Another Brennan–Stebbins means to steal Quarter Circle V."

The obese sheriff sighed. "That's the deal, Kimlock. Quarter Circle V now legally belongs to Silver Brennan an' Deacon Stebbins, the way

161

I understand it. You need to see the county judge, not me."

"You're not lookin' into this rustlin' matter?"

"Not a bit. Hey, what the—"

The sheriff's words were chopped short. You can't speak through a wet hunk of stinking rawhide. Kimlock stood behind the sheriff now, twisting the rawhide tightly around the big head, the sheriff struggling and gasping for breath.

The sheriff's hand went to his holster, but the holster was empty.

Wobbly Head had snaked the sheriff's gun from leather and thrown it out the open back door.

Muffled curses came from within the cowhide. "You might suffocate him to death," Wobbly Head said.

Kimlock grimed. "World'd miss nothin'."

"What's next?"

"Take the shotguns an' rifles from the wall rack. Throw them back in the alley. Then search his desk. Most lawmen keep a pistol or two hidden just for such an emergency as this."

The sheriff kicked, squirmed, hollered—but muffled his yells. Wobbly Head came out of the desk with two pistols which he threw into the alley, also.

"Now lock the door and keep the key. He can't get out to get his guns so fast, with the door locked."

"Door's locked. Key's in my pocket. What do we do next?"

"The next act is mine, brother."

Kimlock's .45 rose. It poised, hesitated, then whacked down, barrel making a sodden sound on the cowhide covering the forepart of the sheriff's big head.

The sheriff immediately stopped struggling. He slumped in his swivel chair, heavy legs spread.

Luke Kimlock unwrapped the cowhide. The sheriff's head dropped onto his thick chest. His eyes were closed. His nostrils moved under heavy breathing. Wobbly Head stared at the unconscious lawman.

"You sure know how to knock a man out, brother."

Luke Kimlock grinned. "I've had a little practice, down along the lawman years."

"How long'll the bastard sleep?"

"About five or six minutes."

"He might come after us a-shootin'."

163

Luke Kimlock shook his head. "I doubt that. I've met his kind before. I'll bet right now he's got Stebbins–Brennan foldin' money in his wallet. An' Stebbins–Brennan dinero in his bank account."

"Everybody knows that, brother. Everybody says this court house is jampacked with crooks and thieves."

"Did you ever see a court house that wasn't?"

"But what if he does come after us?"

Luke Kimlock said, "I'll kill him."

"But what if he kills you?"

Luke Kimlock shrugged. "I'll be dead, that's all."

They went into the long hall. "But let's say you kill him, brother Luke. The county'd be without a sheriff, without law. What'd happen, then?"

"I've seen that happen before in various places. First, do you think any local citizen would fight for the sheriff?"

"Only things like Deacon Stebbins. An' Brennan. An' such low bushwhackers. Why did you ask?"

"Let's say I kill the thing. Outside of the parasites you mentioned, there'd be no opposition—no gun lifted against me."

"How would law be established again?"

Luke Kimlock put his hand on the youth's shoulder. "This is gettin' to be a course in law, brother. Usually the citizens have a town meetin'. They pick a man to head a vigilante commission until an election can be held to replace the killed lawman."

"How about the fink who killed the lawman?"

"Usually he gets a hearin'. And usually he claims self-defense. And usually he's acquitted immediately. Well, here's the county judge's office, the door panel says."

"We goin' in there?"

"We sure are. I want details as to why Uncle Cy was declared mentally incompetent."

"Hooker's the judge. I guess he's been in this court house since the day it was opened, they tell me. Crooked as a snake."

"Most judges are, brother."

They strode in without knocking. A slender oldster wearing black trousers and a white shirt with black sleeve-guards hurriedly came from behind his old desk, plainly the judge's secretary.

"You didn't knock," he said sternly.

"A man never needs to knock entering a

165

county office," Luke Kimlock said. "A county office is owned by the citizens and its door should be open at all times to all people."

"What'd you want?"

"Judge Hooker in?"

"Yes, but—"

"No buts," Luke Kimlock said. "That's all I've heard in this country. Where's he at?"

"In his study. Behin' that door. But—"

The door opened. A tall, bony man of about fifty stood there. "What's going on out here, Mr. Jones?"

The clerk said, "These two men—"

Luke Kimlock cut in with, "Judge Hooker?"

"Yes, I'm Judge Hooker." The gray eyes narrowed. "And you, sir?"

"Luke Kimlock, Cy Blunt's nephew—and legal heir. And my friend is my uncle's closest friend."

"What do you want?"

"Talk to you. In your office."

"Here is good enough and—"

Judge Hooker didn't finish his sentence. Luke Kimlock's big right palm pushed against the judge's pigeon boned breast, forcing the man into his office.

The clerk screamed, "I'll get the sheriff, Judge Hooker."

"Hurry, Jones."

Wobbly Head said to the clerk, "Give the sheriff my regards."

Jones hurried away. Luke Kimlock said, "You stay out here an' guard, brother." He pushed the judge into his big chair. "My uncle has been ruled mentally incompetent. You had a hand in it, bein' you're county judge. On what grounds was this decision reached?"

"Competent and qualified citizens testified as to your uncle's mental instability, Mr. Kimlock."

"Who were these citizens?"

"Their names escape me at the moment. The instrument is on file in the clerk and recorder's office, two doors down the hall on your right. Now, if you'll excuse me—"

Kimlock grinned mirthlessly. "I think two names on that list will be Silver Brennan an' Deacon Stebbins. Yes, and that rat, Doc Miller. This setup has changed lately, I see."

"If you'll—"

"You're not excused, judge. You're in on this swindle, too. When I came to Stirrup City a few days ago Silver Brennan told me he and

167

Deacon Stebbins had got my uncle's ranch on a tax foreclosure sale."

"Tax assessor and collector are down the hall one door, on your left, Mr. Brennan. I'm only county judge."

"You're also a thief," Luke Kimlock said. "A legal thief, judge."

Jones entered, wild-eyed. "Sheriff won't come, judge," he panted. "Said you'd have to take care of it yourself."

"He—what?"

"Jes' as I said, judge."

"I'll have his badge," Judge Hooker said. "Next meetin' of the county commissioners— next Monday—an' he's through."

Wobbly Head giggled. Judge Hooker sent him a hard glance. Jones went to his chair and sat down, watching Kimlock. Kimlock noticed the clerk carefully kept his hands before him on his desk.

Jones wanted nothing to do with this. Kimlock guessed the clerk had a gun in a desk drawer. "Search the clerk's desk," he told Wobbly Head, "an' then look through the judge's drawers."

Wobbly Head smiled. "The one's the judge's wearin', brother, or the ones in his desk?"

"Both."

"Don't put your filthy hands on me!" Judge Hooker told Wobbly Head.

Wobbly Head's search came up with two pistols. Judge Hooker had a Colt .44 and the clerk a Smith and Wesson .38.

"Put them under your belt," Luke Kimlock told the youth. "They might come in handy later on."

"Gift from the county, eh?" Wobbly Head asked.

"Another black mark against you two," Judge Hooker said. "Stealing county property. Serious offense."

Luke Kimlock laughed. "Not as serious as this."

Without warning, his .45 leaped upward, leveled, and, as its owner leaned over the desk in front of the judge, the heavy gun chopped down, barrel cold and deadly.

Judge Hooker hurriedly flung up both arms to protect his head, but he was too late. The .45's barrel landed with a sodden crunch. The judge fell from his swivel chair to the floor, where he didn't move.

Wobbly Head's mouth sagged open in admiration. "Lord in heaven, that was fast, brother.

I mind say you're mite as fast with a gun as that bastardly Deacon Stebbins."

Luke Kimlock looked at Jones. "I want nothin' to do with this," the clerk hurriedly said.

Luke Kimlock counted Jones out. "You saw Stebbins in action, brother?"

"I did. The day he killed the gun quick Texan. The Texan was fast, but Deacon was faster. He ain't human. He's a devil. An' a devil, they tell me, kin move mighty fast."

"Never had anything to do with the devil," Luke Kimlock said. "I ain't a county judge. Let's go."

"Where to?"

"Clerk an' recorders office."

"I'm hungry. Mighty close to noon eatin' time, brother."

"Past noon," Luke Kimlock said. "This won't take long. Then we go somewhere an' put on the nosebag, brother."

"Mike Hanna's the gent to see here," Wobbly Head said. "Uncle Cy cusses Hanna in his sleep claimin' Hanna works in cahoots with Brennan an' Stebbins."

"Uncle Cy told me."

A pretty middle-aged woman was alone in the

170

recorder's office. She reported Mr. Hanna out for dinner. "He should be back soon. Anything I can do for you, sir?"

Kimlock wanted to talk to Hanna. "I'll drop back later, madam, and thanks." The woman showed a nice smile. Kimlock and Wobbly Head went out into the hall. "Only civilized person we've met all day," Wobbly Head said.

They stood on the stone steps. They looked down Beaverton's three block long main street. A block away a young man was hurrying toward the court house on a dog trot.

Down street a rifle spoke. The young man stopped, fell forward on the plank sidewalk, never moved. The rifle's report died.

Luke Kimlock watched carefully, lawman training owning him. All objects, all humans, stood momentarily still, hung suspended on the screen of his mind. The rifle bullet had apparently come from the vacant space between the Express and the Mercantile.

Ambush, Kimlock thought. Dirty ambush.

A running woman dashed into the court house screaming, "Sheriff, sheriff! Mike Hanna —He's been shot!"

"Wonder if he's dead," Wobbly Head asked.

Kimlock said, "He isn't moving, brother.

Looks to me like somebody's beat us to Hanna."

"Ambush, brother."

"That it was," Kimlock said.

The fat sheriff hurried by, the townswoman following him. As the lawman passed Kimlock said dryly, "Get on your cayuse, you fat bastard! Earn your pay!"

The sheriff sent a hate filled glance in his direction, but said nothing. They carried Hanna into the Apple Barrel Saloon, Hanna's body a broken sack.

"Looks dead to me," Wobbly Head said.

Kimlock shrugged. "Hard to tell."

The sheriff had gone into the space between the store and the newspaper office. He came out with a rifle. Kimlock and Wobbly Head stood on the court-house steps and watched.

A small boy came by. "Mr. Hanna dead?" Kimlock asked.

"Plumb dead, mister. Bullet tore off the top of his head. Rifle belonged to Seeger. Carl Seeger, the name on the end of the rifle said."

"Who's Carl Seeger?" Kimlock asked.

"Bum who drifts in an' outa town. Comes an' goes. Sheriff's lookin' for him now."

"Looks as if he's found him," Kimlock said,

and the boy turned to see the fat sheriff fairly dragging a handcuffed young man from a saloon beyond the Apple Barrel.

"This ain't logical," Wobbly Head said.

Luke Kimlock nodded.

"When a man kills a man from ambush, he don't stick aroun' to walk into jail."

"The guy there's not walkin' into jail," Luke Kimlock murmured. "He's bustin' into jail."

"He looks drunk to me," Kimlock said.

"Maybe he don't remember what he did?"

Luke Kimlock shook his head. "I've heard of people bein' that drunk but I never could believe it. I've been looped on my boots a few times but I always remember what I did."

Wobbly Head's eyes narrowed. "If I mind right, Mike Hanna was Uncle Sam's boy for homestead entries and such. And Uncle Cy had all that land homestead by his cowpunchers and he paid them well and now them homesteads belong to Brennan an' Stebbins?"

"That's what I understand."

"Uncle Cy's really gettin' a workin' over," Wobbly Head said.

"Not for long," Luke Kimlock said. "All will be righted inside of a few days."

"Hope you're right, brother Luke."

"I'm right. An' what is more—Hey, where you goin'?"

"I'll be right back." Wobbly Head entered the court house. "Got to see a man about a horse, brother."

Luke Kimlock pushed back his Stetson. Luke Kimlock scratched his head.

13

WOBBLY HEAD did not stop inside the court house. He went straight through the building to exit by the rear door into the alley. He hurried down the alley to the Circle Diamond barn.

Evidently the hostler was out on main street watching the proceedings for only horses inhabited the barn. Wobbly Head stopped behind a big blue roan gelding.

The horse bore a Circle S brand. Despite this, Wobbly Head knew the bronc belonged to Circle Diamond.

He also knew Circle Diamond kept saddle broncs on its Buggy Creek linecamp. The thing was simple. Neefy had changed broncs at Buggy Creek. Neefy was in Beaverton.

Wobbly Head then looked at the saddles on the racks. He immediately identified Neefy's Miles City kak, a swell-forked outfit, single rig. He also noticed that Neefy's rifle rode in its saddle boot, polished walnut stock sticking upward.

But one thing for sure: Neefy was in Beaverton. And, with Neefy in town, Luke Kimlock's life was in danger.

Wobbly Head also guessed that Neefy had killed Mike Hanna. Neefy'd ambushed Hanna to silence him forever. He'd been afraid Mike Hanna might have broken under Kimlock pressure.

Wobbly Head also reasoned that Brennan or Stebbins had ordered Neefy to kill Mike Hanna. Stebbins and Brennan had apparently used Mike Hanna as much as they'd been able.

And, not being able to use Hanna and Hanna's office more, they'd sent Neefy to Beaverton to eliminate Mike Hanna, which apparently Neefy had done with a stolen rifle.

Wobbly Head did some more thinking. He was sure that Brennan and Stebbins knew Luke Kimlock was in Beaverton. Circle Diamond had spies across the entire country and one of these would have surely seen him and Luke Kimlock leave Stirrup Basin range yesterday and would have reported same to their bosses, of course.

He shivered despite the heat. Neefy would next kill Luke Kimlock. That was as sure as the sun would rise tomorrow morning.

Wobbly Head's world consisted of only two

elements. One was his love for horseflesh. He could take the toughest, meanest Montana bronc and within a month through love and care could be mounted on the brute cutting cattle.

His second love: Uncle Cy Blunt.

Standing there, he remembered his orphanage. Alone, hungry, facing Omaha's terribly hot summer days, shivering under its driving blizzards. Nobody had wanted him. Nobody had loved him. And then he'd accidentally met Uncle Cy. And the whole world had changed.

Somebody had wanted him. Somebody had loved him. He'd suddenly become necessary to somebody. And when Uncle Cy had settled on Stirrup River and had gone to Omaha after him—Wobbly Head choked on emotion. One thing stood out clearly—with Luke Kimlock dead, Uncle Cy would really be finished. And Neefy was in this town—prowling the alleys, snarling, killer-mad and Neefy would kill Luke Kimlock. And then where would Uncle Cy and Wobbly Head be?

No, he'd have to kill Neefy. And kill the thin lipped, sallow gunman before that gunman could ambush and kill Luke Kimlock.

But where would he begin?

His own saddle-boot carried a loaded Winchester .30–30, the gift of Uncle Cy. He needed that rifle. He packed a .45 Colts on his hip. He'd need that short gun, too.

Wobbly Head hurried to the livery barn where he and Luke Kimlock had left their horses. He pulled his rifle from saddle scabbard.

His rifle, a Henry .44 caliber repeater was old but reliable, a gift from Uncle Cy. He never carried a bullet under the exposed hammer, for the hammer might catch on something and cause an accident but he always kept the long magazine loaded with fifteen cartridges.

The rifle was a bit shorter than he was, but its twenty-four inch barrel allowed for fairly accurate shooting at long range, experience had taught him for he'd toppled quite a few coyotes and buck deers with the repeater. He patted it absently, brow furrowed in thought.

He had the desire to kill Neefy. He had the equipment to kill the gunman. But where was Neefy?

You had to find a man before you could kill him.

Neefy drank a lot, Wobbly Head knew. Therefore he hung out around saloons. He liked the women. Saloons usually had cribs upstairs. Was Neefy upstairs in some Beaverton saloon with a woman?

Wobbly Head smiled. He wished he were a hawk. Then he could fly over Beaverton and see clearly all that happened below, men moving on the streets, riders going back and forth.

And he could hover in and look into upstairs windows, too. The boy smiled at such a foolish thought. Carrying his rifle, he walked out into the brilliant, hot Montana sunshine.

He looked up and down Beaverton's main street. Being the county seat, Beaverton therefore was much bigger than Stirrup City; about three times the people, he'd heard.

The court house fronted one end of main street, sitting in its circle, the road going around it. The community church occupied the circle at the south end of main street, its high belfry sticking up into the cloudless blue sky.

The thought came to Wobbly Head that the church's belfry was the highest point in Beaverton. Again, he remembered thinking of a hawk. He didn't have wings, but he did have the belfry.

But how to get up into it?

He went toward the church, carrying his old

179

rifle. He did not walk the main street; he clung to the alley. He came in from behind on the frame building. He halted in the willows beside the creek that meandered around Beaverton to enter Stirrup River just west of town.

A cowboy rode by, singing an old trail song. Wobbly Head remained hidden in the high buckbrush. The parson lived in a modest house behind his church. He came out and accosted the cowboy, who reined in and talked with the angular, bony preacher.

Wobbly Head impatiently waited. He heard the conversation. The preacher wanted the cowboy to bring him in some fresh venison. The preacher had a wife and five children, Wobbly learned.

Finally, the cowboy rode on. The preacher entered his house. The yard back of the church was deserted. From downtown Beaverton came the sounds of men calling and talking.

Wobbly Head looked at the open door of the church. To get into the church he'd have to cross the strip between the church and the parson's house. The parson's door was open and that side of the house had two windows. Wobbly Head's heart beat heavily.

Surely the parson or some of his family,

would see him cross that area. Wobbly Head then remembered seeing a bunch of town children heading for the creek to swim when he'd come up the alley. He didn't recognize all the young ones in the group but he did remember seeing three of the parson's get in the gang. Maybe only the preacher and his wife were in the house?

He pulled air into his lungs. His palms were damp on the rifle's stock. He had to take a chance. If the preacher or somebody called out, he'd say he was only crossing the circle to get on the other side.

His boots ground gravel. Evidently the preacher had tried to grow grass in the circle for a few tufts of green showed despite the dry season.

He carried his rifle, barrel uppermost, in front of his body, thereby hoping to hide it, for he knew the preacher was very much against a man packing a lethal weapon; in fact, the minister had recently appeared before the Beaverton town council advocating a no weapon law within the city limits.

Uncle Cy had told him that. A no weapon law meant nobody within Beaverton's city limits could pack a rifle or short gun. Upon entering

181

town, a cowboy'd have to check his weapons in at a public checking-station.

According to Uncle Cy, the preacher's measure had missed passage by a mere one vote in the ten man town council.

Wobbly Head wondered why he thought such unimportant thoughts at this ticklish moment. He realized he had covered about half the distance to the church's open door. His heart beat loudly. He could hear it in his ears. Any minute he expected a voice to call out to him from the house.

His boots seemed to ring unnecessarily loud on the steel steps. Within a few minutes, he was stationed in the high lookout, Beaverton spread out below him with its frame buildings and dusty roads and plank sidewalks and horses tied patiently to hitchracks in front of saloons and other establishments.

Wobby Head's eyes narrowed. He saw Luke Kimlock. Luke entered a building on the east side of the street. Wobbly Head figured the building housed railroad officials. Luke evidently was going in to have it out with the railroad bigwigs about running rails across land that Stebbins and Brennan now claimed but

182

which legally—in Wobbly Head's mind—still belonged to Uncle Cy.

Would Luke have to slug unconscious another high bigshot official, as he'd done to the sheriff and Judge Hooker?

Then, he saw something suspicious. A man walked across a flat roof on a building well past the middle of main street. The building was on the west side of the thoroughfare, directly opposite the railroad office's front door.

Wobbly Head's heart leaped in his scrawny chest, for the man was nobody else but Neefy. Gripping his rifle, the boy stared downward, blood pounding—yes, it was Neefy. It had to be Neefy!

Wobbly Head stared, seeing the man clearly. The man doffed his Stetson and wiped his forehead with a red bandana. Wobbly Head realized it was very hot on the flat, tarred roof.

Rifle ready, he waited.

Time ran by. Flies droned. A mosquito found him even on his high perch. It had a stinger half a foot long, it seemed. He batted it on his neck. He killed it. A bit of blood came back on his hand.

More time dribbled past. Men moved, women went to market, kids came from swimming, went to the creek to swim. Riders moved back and forth below, some coming, some leaving.

Finally, the door of the railroad office opened. Wobbly Head was on his feet, rifle rising—and then he saw the man leaving was not Luke Kimlock, so he settled back again.

The ambusher on the roof settled back, also, Wobbly Head noticed. He'd risen also, rifle coming up and then, recognition evidently coming in, he'd lowered his weapon again and again sunk to a crouch behind the roof's parapet.

Again, the Quarter Circle V waif waited. Again, came mosquitos, two this time, both meeting instant and ignoble deaths. The heat grew. Flies buzzed. And then, again the door opened.

This time, Luke Kimlock walked out.

Kneeling, Neefy slanted his rifle over the parapet, aiming down at Luke Kimlock. Hurriedly, Wobbly Head's Henry's sights found Neefy. He had very little time. He used it rapidly.

His hammer fell. The cartridge exploded. Evidently Neefy pulled trigger just a shade behind. Wobbly Head's bullet fell short. It hit the parapet a foot from Neefy's rifle.

Wobbly Head saw concrete dust jet upward. For the first time, Neefy apparently realized a rifle was higher than his rifle. He straightened. That made him visible over the false-front from Luke Kimlock, standing below. Neefy turned. He stared momentarily up at the church's steeple, rifle rising.

Wobbly Head had his control, now. He shot again, head against the sleek stock, hammer falling. A bullet plowed into the steeple to his right, scattering wooden splinters.

This time, the boy shot true. Neefy took the bullet. He dropped his rifle. He staggered. He fell over the false front. He disappeared.

Wobbly Head shot a glance at Luke Kimlock, still standing in front of the railroad's office. Kimlock had his .45 in his hand. Wobbly Head saw sunlight glisten from the blued steel. Neefy's hastily flung lead had apparently gone wild.

Then, even as the boy watched, Luke Kimlock glanced up at the steeple, then started walking across the street toward Neefy. He holstered his .45 as he walked. That told

Wobbly Head that Neefy was out of commission as a gunman.

Had he killed Neefy?

Wobbly Head had no time to waste. Below him the preacher and his wife hurried down street. Wobbly Head ran down the stairs, openly out the back door and was soon at the barn where he restored his rifle to saddle scabbard.

The barn held no humans. All of Beaverton was gathered around Neefy when Wobbly Head arrived. He tugged Luke Kimlock's shirtsleeve. "What happened, brother?"

"Neefy was up on this roof. He aimed to ambush me when I come out of the railroad's office yonderly. Somebody shot him. He fell dead to the planks."

"He aimed to kill you from the roof, eh? Ambush, again."

"That's the way I read it, boy."

"Who shot him? And from where?"

Luke Kimlock suddenly studied the boy. "Where you been?"

"Down the crick. Swimmin'. I got hot."

"Swimmin', huh? Why ain't your hair wet?"

"Kept my head above water, that's why. I get water in my eyes and they swell up turibly.

186

I asked you a coupla questions. So far I ain't got no answers, brother."

"I don't know where the bullet that killed him came from. An' I don't know who fired it."

"I don't understand, brother."

Again, Luke Kimlock looked at the youth. "I'll talk to you in private, brother—too many people aroun' now."

"Talk about what?"

A man said, "Bullet come from direction of the church, I think. Anyway, this dead man turned, fired toward the church."

"How'd you know? Was you on a roof?" somebody asked.

"I was on the Merc's roof. Fixin' a leak."

Somebody said, "Don't reckon the parson's takin' to shootin' down gunmen, do you?" He laughed. "This gent slung a gun for them two bastards west in Stirrup City. Stebbins an' Brennan."

"I didn't shoot him," the minister said. "I'm in the saving end, not the destructive end."

Luke Kimlock introduced himself. "I'm Cy Blunt's nephew. I figure Brennan an' Stebbins sent Neefy into town to ambush an' kill me."

A man put his hand on Wobbly Head's

shoulder. "Maybe your partner here gunned him down." He spoke jokingly.

"Heck, yes," Wobbly Head said, smiling. "I'm the guilty one."

They all laughed. Seemingly no tears would be shed over the dead Neefy. The sheriff looked at Kimlock. "You care to deliver his carcass to Stirrup City, sir? County will pay the expense, Mr. Kimlock?"

Wobbly Head hid his smile. Now it was SIR and MR. "We'll do that, sheriff," Kimlock said. "We were jes' ready to leave town, anyway, business all completed. I got a hunch this dead gent ambushed your Mike Hanna, too."

The sheriff rubbed his jaw. "Sounds logical. Well, get him a horse an' outa Beaverton, huh?"

Soon Luke Kimlock and Wobbly Head rode out of town heading west, the body of Neefy jackknifed across the saddle of the blue roan, hands tied to the off cinch ring so the carcass wouldn't slide from saddle.

"How'd you come out with the railroad bigwigs?" Wobbly Head asked.

"They haven't bought right-of-way off Stebbins an' Brennan yet. They know about the trouble between them two hellions an' Uncle Cy and they're layin' low."

"What if they start to lay steel on one of Uncle Cy's homesteads?"

Luke Kimlock shrugged. "Rifles and short-guns, I'd say. I think we'd best ride the trip in one session. This heat'll make ol' Neefy bloat up an' start to stink."

"Whoever kilt him should've done it aroun' evenin' time, for evenin's are much cooler," Wobbly Head said.

"Who'd you figure killed him?"

"I dunno."

"You sure you don't?"

"Damn sure, brother."

They rode on. Ten miles further west they met the Quarter Circle V rider heading east, whipping his lathered bronc down the hind legs.

"Where you headed for?" Luke Kimlock asked.

"Beaverton. An' for you, Luke. Brennan an' Stebbins—They found the mouth of your tunnel—"

Luke Kimlock's heart sank.

"They killed the guard there. They came up from the basement—about twenty of 'em—"

"Hurry, man!"

"They took us by su'prise. I escaped by luck, nothin' more. Silver Brennan was with 'em. An' Silver Brennan killed your Uncle Cy!"

Wobbly Head wailed, "Oh, lord, no!"

Luke Kimlock's mouth held dry ash.

14

THAT night Deacon Stebbins loved his violin, a soft smile on his thin lips. Everything had gone right. Uncle Cy Blunt had been killed. Now all of Stirrup Basin range was his and Silver Brennan's.

Silver Brennan . . .

His smile widened. Silver Brennan didn't have long to live, although the saloon man didn't know that.

His bow danced across the strings. Savage and deadly, the music; a German war-song, and the Prussians dueled, steel clashing against steel. And the sounds moved out the open window and across the sun-beaten, storm-lashed buildings of this frontier cowtown.

Townsmen stopped. They listened. The madame on Brennan's second floor listened, lips compressed. The music bothered her. She ordered her girls to close their windows despite the cloyish, clinging heat.

"He's happy," a red-head told the madame.

"Don't sound that way to me, honey."

"Circle Diamond raided Quarter Circle V," the red-head said. "Haven't you heard? Brennan and Stebbins drove Blunt men from their ranch. And the old man—Uncle Cy—was killed."

"There's still his nephew, that Kimlock man."

"The one who knocked the boss through the Steerhorn's door, glass and all? '

"That's Kimlock."

"He's only one. Brennan an' Deacon; they've got lots of guns hired. Neefy, for one."

"Haven't seen Neefy for a day or so," the madame said.

"He'll show up soon," the red-head said. "He always does, sooner or later. This is my last night here, Gertie. When mornin' comes I'm on the stage to Hangton."

"Why? You turn a lot of tricks here. Railroad crews have lotsa money."

"I'm afraid, Gertie."

Gertie nodded. "I understand, Emilie. I've felt it in the air. The town down't like us. If Brennan an' Deacon started to fall—I've seen it before. And it wasn't fun. I was ridden out of town on a rail, tarred and feathered. I still got scars from the hot tar."

"I'm gettin' out, Gertie."

"Listen to that damn violin!"

For the violin had taken on even a more strident, arrogant note. For the pitch was rising, coming up and up, building and adding and cutting knife-like across the dark night air.

Deacon Stebbins sat in dim lamplight, his shadow thrown across the closed window drape. The shadow moved, the violin sobbed and threatened and Deacon Stebbins smiled softly, eyes dreamy and soft for once.

All had turned out well.

Neefy was in Beaverton. A courier had brought back word that Mike Hanna had been ambushed and killed by a drunken Beaverton cowhand. Any time now the other courier stationed in Beaverton should bring in word that Neefy had eliminated, for once and for always, that damned nephew, Luke Kimlock.

Everything had worked out correctly. With Kimlock dead, all this range would be his . . . after Brennan was eliminated. The violin rang out its pitched song of victory.

He thought of Cy Blunt's will in the safe below in his bank, secure and doctored. He went over essentials. All was well here in

Stirrup City and Stirrup Basin. Accordingly he wasted thoughts on his day's success.

His thoughts centered around Beaverton.

The fat, bumbling sheriff. He had him in his pocket. He and Silver Brennan paid the sheriff more each month than the sheriff drew from the county in wages.

But it was money well spent. The territory had laws against prostitution. The saloon took in enough in two ordinary nights to pay the sheriff's wages and leave over a few bucks besides.

The sheriff was paid NOT to have a deputy stationed in Stirrup City. Therefore no lawman could, or would, interfere in any way. He and Silver Brennan had the run of the town.

Playing softly now, Deacon Stebbins let his thoughts momentarily settle on the residents of Stirrup City. On this point, he wasn't sure and his gaunt, savage face, outlined by yellow lamplight, showed this fact.

He realized he'd erred when he'd shot O'Rourke in the saddle. His temper had got the best of him, a thing he seldom allowed. Spies reported certain townspeople were shocked by the cold-blooded daylight murder, among these being Doc Miller.

If Townspeople threatened to rise up he'd get the Beaverton sheriff to send a deputy to Stirrup City—a deputy who, of course, would be under control of Circle Diamond. The deputy would keep the citizens in line.

Deacon Stebbins' thoughts returned to Beaverton. Judge Israel Hooker . . . Judge Hooker also drew more money from Circle Diamond than he did from the county.

The banker smiled, violin dancing again. All was safe. Soon a courier would ride in telling of Luke Kimlock's ambushing and being killed. Or Neefy himself—triumphant, snickering, sneering—would bring the news in person.

Deacon Stebbins went to sleep in his chair. He was awakened shortly by the guard pounding on his door and asking him to unlock it so Silver Brennan could enter.

Using a double-barreled twelve-gauge shotgun as a crutch, the banker hobbled to the door and turned the key, then hobbled back to his chair, anger scrawled across his thin face. The guard shut the door behind Brennan and went below.

"What eats you, Brennan?"

"Mullins jus' rode in from Beaverton.

195

Kimlock pole axed both the sheriff an' the judge."

"He—what?"

"Slugged both with his six-shooter barrel."

"What then happened?"

"Nothin'."

Deacon Stebbins studied his partner. "What'd you mean by NOTHING?"

"Jus' what I said. Nothin' more happened. Hooker an' the sheriff refused to press the thing further an' arrest Kimlock."

"Why?"

"Scared of him, I reckon."

"Neefy?"

"Not a word more about him. Mullins reported that the sheriff acts friendly toward Kimlock, now. An' the sheriff don't know, or seem to care to fin' out who gunned down Mike Hanna."

Deacon Stebbins nodded, eyes thoughtful. "Mullins didn't say anythin' about Kimlock goin' under?"

"Not a word. When he left Beaverton, Kimlock was still on his pins, he says."

"What time did he leave?"

"I don't know. Never asked him. Forty miles away. Good hoss like Mullins rides should cover that distance inside of four hours—no, less than that time, if pushed. He left somewhere aroun' five, I'd reckon."

"It all depends on Neefy," Deacon Stebbins said.

Silver Brennan nodded. "An' if Neefy fails?"

"It then shifts over to you, Brennan."

"I'd be pleased," Silver Brennan said.

Deacon Stebbins laughed. "Would you NOW, Silver?" His words dripped sarcasm. "You didn't do so good the day Kimlock came into town."

"Don't rub me in the wrong direction, Deacon," Silver Brennan warned.

Again, a sardonic laugh.

Silver Brennan strode to the window. He parted the drapes to look down on Stirrup City and its lamplight. He spoke over a shoulder. "Mullins said this Kimlock button sent out telegrams to various territorial police, and state police, askin' about our past lives, Deacon."

"Where'd he send them out?"

"Beaverton, of course. Railroad wire."

"They never got out of Beaverton," Deacon Stebbins said. "Those depot agents there, the telegraphers . . . they know who helps pay their big wages, and they don't forget."

"Hope you're right."

"What else did Mullins say?"

"Kimlock talked with the railroad officials. He don't know what they talked about, of course but I suppose it was right-of-way grants. I don't know what he learned, naturally."

"He learned nothing. They're tight mouthed. They're not our friends, they're not his. They just want right-of-way. They don't care who they buy it from just so the sale is cheap enough."

"And legal?"

"Legality means nothin' to those bastards! They're a big, money-grabbing corporation, with Uncle Sam on their side or else why would Uncle give them every other section of gover'ment land free on each side of their rails? Uncle's given those thieves millions and millions of acres."

"That's all I know, Deacon."

"That was enough."

Silver Brennan left. Deacon Stebbins sat in his chair, head cocked, listening to the saloon man's boots slowly descend the outer stairs. Silver Brennan walked slowly.

Deacon Stebbins smiled. Brennan was worried. That was good. When a man was worried, he was more alert. A worried man expected something serious to happen. When it did, worry had made him more prepared.

Deacon Stebbins raised his violin, struck three notes, then lowered the instrument. He was not in the mood. Brennan might have worries but he had none. His head dropped. Pain fell away before benevolent sleep, but his sojourn in the arms of Morpheus was again disturbed by Silver Brennan.

"For Lord's sake, Deacon, let me in!"

Deacon Stebbins again hobbled on his shotgun crutch to the door. Again, the heavy key turned, the heavy door opened; again, an agitated Silver Brennan pushed in, shutting the door in the guard's face. The guard returned below to his shot gun station.

Lamplight showed an agitated saloon man. "Now what the hell's wrong?" Deacon Stebbins growled.

"Neefy, Deacon. Neefy's dead."

Deacon Stebbins hobbled back to his chair. He sat down laboriously, teeth gritted against pain. For some moments, pain held him without words, but finally he asked, "Give me details, please."

Brennan told about Neefy's death in

Beaverton. "Luke Kimlock an' that Quarter Circle V halfwit—that Wobbly Head—they toted the carcass in from Beaverton tied over Neefy's own horse."

"Who killed Neefy?"

"Nobody seems to know."

"Nobody knows?" Deacon Stebbins stared at his partner. "How come they don't know?"

Brennan explained that angle. "Some claim the bullet thet kilt Neefy came from the church tower, but nobody's sure."

Deacon Stebbins scowled. "From the church tower? That doesn't make sense, man. How'd you know all this? Who brought Neefy's body into town?"

"Smith."

"Who the hell is Smith?"

"Martin Smith. Thet cowpuncher who works for us. You remember him, don't you?"

Deacon Stebbins dimly remembered Smith. "How come he get hold of Neefy?" he asked.

"Smith met Kimlock an' this halfwit a couple of miles out of town, along Doggone Crick. Kimlock turned the carcass over to Smith to take to town."

"Nice of him," Deacon Stebbins said.

"What's that piece of paper you got there in your hand?"

"Oh, I almost forgot. Kimlock sent this in with Smith."

Brennan handed the note to Stebbins.

"Where's Kimlock now?" Stebbins asked.

"Smith said he an' the nut rid toward Quarter Circle V, after Smith tol' him his Uncle Cy's carcass had been taken there by our gunmen after they cleaned Quarter Circle V outa our ranch."

"What does the note say?"

"Best you read it, Deacon."

Shot gun crutch punching the thick carpet, the banker hobbled to the kerosene lamp, note in hand. He turned up the wick, the lamp responding. He held the note close to the chimney, the neatly-written words coming out clearly.

He read aloud:

Stebbins, Brennan, to wit:
Brennan murdered my uncle. I am going to kill you both, Brennan and Stebbins. I've decided to use dynamite. It is fast, deadly, and instantly destructive. I am going to blow up the bank to get my uncle's will from the

safe. I'm going to blow up Brennan's saloon, too. I'm setting no date. Stew in your own worries, you bastards. Stick with your bank and saloon, and up you go in flames.

Signed,
Luke Kimlock.

15

NEXT sundown they buried Uncle Cy Blunt and the dead Quarter Circle V cowboys in the cemetery on the hill overlooking the cow outfit's dynamited buildings, the Beaverton traveling preacher conducting the ceremony, Montana's ever present wind whipping the long tails of his black frock coat.

"Let us pray, gentlemen."

Luke bowed his head, throat tight. Wobbly Head stood at his right. Wobbly Head's eyes were blank, his lips compressed. He'd taken Uncle Cy's murder hard. Upon hearing of his benefactor's passing he'd wanted to ride straight into Stirrup City and match his gun against those of Deacon Stebbins and Silver Brennan.

He'd wheeled his bronc's head toward Stirrup City, screaming curses against Brennan and Stebbins. Luke had tackled him and dragged him from leather, throwing the boy on his back in the sagebrush.

"Boy, lissen to me, dang your hide!"

"Brother Luke, let me up or—"

"Or you'll do nothin'," Luke had ordered. "You don't ride into Stirrup City, remember?"

"Brennan—Deacon Stebbins—They sent out the gunman who murdered Uncle Cy—"

"You ride into town an' you'll be workin' right into their hands, boy. You'll run into more than the fast guns of Brennan an' Stebbins."

"I know that, brother Luke."

"You'll never get to match lead with Brennan. Or with Stebbins. Their gunnies will cut you down fast and pronto first. All you'll be doin' is committin' suicide!"

"Luke's right," the Quarter Circle V cowpuncher said.

Luke said, gently, "Use your noodle, Brother Elmer. Quiet down, please."

"But Brennan—Uncle Cy—with his shoulder —He couldn't even pull a gun, brother!"

"I know that."

"It was murder, brother! Cold-blooded murder!"

"I know that too, brother," Luke had said, "but you're not going off half-cocked and in the mental shape you're in. I can't let you commit suicide, boy."

"Then what can we do?"

"Use our heads," Luke Kimlock said.

Wobbly Head stared upward, moonlight showing his wide, ugly face. Then, without warning, he began to weep.

Luke got to his feet.

Now, watching the coffin go into the Montana soil, Luke Kimlock realized he held no great sorrow because of his uncle's untimely death. Uncle Cy had lived quite a number of years.

He'd lived a good life. He'd not been penned in by four walls. He'd been tied to no particular job. He'd gone to this town, then that, this ranch, then that, buying cattle.

He'd lived a life many a city man would have given his wealth to live, Luke Kimlock reasoned.

Luke Kimlock realized that now this range belonged to him. Uncle Cy's will had so stated, the only thing in doubt was this: How could he lay his hands on the will?

Luke Kimlock had been a law officer all his adult life. He knew there were ways to prove whether or not a signature was authentic or a fraud. Also a police laboratory could prove erasures in a document and the difference between one signature and the signature of another.

He needed that will. And when Luke Kimlock needed something, Luke Kimlock invariably got what he searched for.

"We ain't even got a roof over our heads," Wobbly Head said.

Luke Kimlock looked at the dynamited buildings below. "We'll rebuild, boy. Have faith."

"Faith . . . and fast guns," the boy added.

Luke nodded. He was patting down Uncle Cy's grave with the back of his spade. The parson had gone on to preach over the other Quarter Circle V men the Brennan-Stebbins raid had killed.

Quarter Circle V had lost four in the gunfight, including Uncle Cy. Luke Kimlock found grim satisfaction in the fact that roaring Quarter Circle V guns had killed six Circle Diamond gunmen.

Brennan had gone through the gunsmoke battle unharmed.

"After buryin' good ol' Smokey—an' Bill—an' Hans—Well, what's next, brother Luke? Do we ride into town an' fight it out with

Brennan an' Stebbins an' their gunhan's?" Wobbly Head asked.

Luke Kimlock shook his head.

"You turnin' white feather, brother Luke?"

Luke leaned on his long-handled shovel. "There are times when I wonder just what you pack for brains in that skull of yours, boy. Sawdust?"

"I don't foller you."

"All right, say we ride into town. You know what'll happen. Stebbins an' Brennan'll have the town spiked against us with rifles an' short guns. Men behin' rain barrels on the street corners behin' false front buildin's Rifles an' pistols hidden an' firin' from the top of Brennan's saloon—from the upstairs windows in Stebbins' bank."

"Then what does we do?"

"We make them come to us, an' on our terms."

"How'd we do that?"

"You ask a lot of questions."

"How?"

"Wait and see," Luke said.

The burials finished, Luke slipped the parson an eagle, then escorted the man of God to his buggy. He returned to his men, the parson's rig going down hill, heading toward Stirrup City where he would spend the night.

Circle Diamond had no need for the parson's kind words. Circle Diamond had buried its dead without benefit of a clergyman's soothing words in the section of Stirrup City's public cemetery reserved for Circle Diamond.

Luke pointed north down on Stirrup River's cottonwood trees. "We bunk tonight in that bunch of trees directly west of the ranch's buildings," he told his small crew.

They trooped down hill, carrying shovels and rifles and leading cowponies. Once in the thick grove, Luke stationed guards—two men moving on endless patrol in the brush—and called the rest of Uncle Cy's crew to be seated.

Cowhands sat with backs against trees. Luke went right to the point. How many wanted revenge on Circle Diamond? Those who didn't want to stay with Quarter Circle V could ride out unmolested, he assured.

"I'd see your point of view. The man who bossed the iron that paid you wages is dead. You're loyalty naturally would be toward the man, not toward the iron he burned into cowhide."

Cowpokes listened, some chewing stems of

208

grass, others just watching in silence. Luke counted only nine hands including himself and Wobbly Head and the two on guard.

"How many want to leave?" he asked.

Two men stood up. "Sorry," one said, "but I can't see us winnin', 'cause the odds ag'in us are jus' too big."

"Okay, Cummins. I see your point-of-view. How much does the ranch owe you?"

"Not a cent, Luke."

"You get paid," Luke said shortly. "Uncle Cy'd want it that way. How many days, Cummins?"

"Dang it, Luke, I don't want Uncle Cy's money!"

Luke gave in. "As you say, Cummins."

"I ain't ridin' my own horse," Cummins said. "My saddle critter bears Quarter Circle V's iron."

"You're ridin' your own horse now," Luke Kimlock told the cowpuncher. "I give you the bronc."

"I'd appreciate a bill-of-sale, Luke. Some lawman might stop me an' want proof."

"Who's got a pencil an' a piece of paper?" Luke asked.

A cowpuncher had a stub of pencil and a

209

piece of dirty paper. Luke wrote, "Sold on this day—Hell, what day is it, men?"

Nobody knew.

"Okay, I'll not put a date, just the year," Luke said. The document finished, he handed it to Cummins who pocketed it, smiled sheepishly at all concerned, and mounted and rode out, heading west toward Hangton and the mining area.

Luke looked at the second quitter, a tall slim youth of about twenty. "I got a wife an' a little baby, Luke, holdin' down a homestead for me right out of Beaverton. I'd like to stay, if I was single, I'd have my gun right 'longside of yours but that little buster baby of mine needs a daddy, Luke."

"I understan', Beavens. Wobbly Head pointed out your young missus an' baby to me in Beaverton. They'd hiked into town for a mite of supplies, your wife tol' me. Good luck, boy."

"Same to you, Mr. Kimlock. An' the rest of you boys. I ride my own saddler, Mr. Kimlock. An' like Cummins, Uncle Cy don't owe me a cent."

"You're gettin' paid," Luke insisted. "Cummins has no kin; you have. Thet baby needs, Beavens."

"Well, if you insist."

"I insist," Luke Kimlock said. "How many days?"

Beavens counted on his fingers. Luke paid him in silver and gold dug from his Levi's pocket. Soon Beavens rode out but he headed east toward Beaverton. Luke looked at his crew of seven, counting Wobbly Head. "The rest of you stay?"

"Till the last dog's cut and rope hung," one said.

Luke said, "Thanks, boys. The two on guard —Martin and Rivers—said they'd stay, too."

His gaze traveled from cowpuncher to cowpuncher. A sense of dismay hit him. It would be seven against the many Stebbins-Brennan gunmen. But it had to be done and, in his estimation, there was only one way to do it, a plan he now outlined. "We boycott Stirrup City," he explained.

"Boycott," Wobbly Head said. "What does that word mean, brother Luke?"

"It means we allow nobody into Stirrup City nor do we allow anybody out. That's it in a simple manner, boy."

"You mean we starve them to givin' up?" a cowpuncher asked.

211

Luke nodded. "No grub goes in. Nothin' enters. Nothin' leaves."

"How do we do that?" another waddy asked.

"We close the road in. There are only two. One from Beaverton; t'other from Hangton."

"Be tough on the citizens inside," Wobbly Head said. "I gotta hunch quite a passle would be on our side if they wasn't so 'fraid of Deacon Stebbins an' Silver Brennan."

"That's what we want, Wobbly Head."

"What'd you mean by that?"

"If they're on our side—an' they're penned in because of Brennan an' Stebbins—well, they'll turn against the two, won't they?"

"Good idea, brother Luke."

Then began one of the strangest events that ever took place in the Territory of Montana. Quarter Circle V's seven riders circled Stirrup City, keeping hidden by brush and keeping all except the town herd of milk cows within the perimeters of the pioneer town.

"The milk cows an' the kid herdin' them can get through," Luke Kimlock told his riders, "'cause we aim to starve the grown ups into a rebellion ag'in Brennan an' Stebbins, not starve babies to death.

The two stagecoaches one headed from

Beaverton to Hangton and the one making the return trip were not allowed to enter town or put off freight or mail or passengers.

"The sheriff'll tend to you," the driver told Luke Kimlock.

"Send him out," Kimlock said, "an' I'll send a bullet through his fat belly jus' to lissen to the gas escape, an' I'll bet the gas will be hot, too."

"Judge Hooker'll hear about this," the other driver threatened.

"He come out here," Luke Kimlock said, "an' I'll kill him, an' he knows it—an' so does your sheriff."

"I got to get out," a young girl said. "I'm going to work for Silver Brennan."

"You won't get out here, miss," Luke Kimlock said. "Travel on to Hangton. I've heard the houses there need new girls."

Another painted girl stuck out her head and tongue. "You sonofabitch," she said.

The Hangton stage carried gold bullion the third day headed for the railhead and shipment east. A shotgun guard rode the boot along with the regular driver. "We need fresh hosses, mister," the burly guard told Luke Kimlock, "an' Stirrup City's got 'em."

"What'd you aim to do?"

"Drive in an' change teams."

Luke Kimlock shook his head. "You don't do it, guard. You push on. Nobody leaves or enters Stirrup City."

The guard raised his shotgun slightly. "We do, Mister Kimlock."

Kimlock and Wobbly Head shot at the same time. The shotgun went flying, a bullet hitting its double barrel, another smashing its stock. The guard stared at his numbed, shaking fingers.

"That convince you?" Kimlock asked.

The guard's voice was shaky. "It sure does, mister. Can you hand me up my scattergun, please?"

Luke picked up the weapon. He jacked it open, ejected the twin shells, then shoved sand in the two barrels before handing it, shattered stock and all, upward.

"Keep it as a souvenir," Luke said dryly.

The stage driver cracked his lash over the backs of his sweaty four horses. The stage rocked on east.

"You're a dead shot, brother Luke."

Luke grinned. "You're not so bad yourself, brother Elmer."

The fifth day, Doctor Henry Miller walked out of town, carrying high a white towel on a long stick.

"Town's running out of grub, Kimlock."

"Cook Brennan an' Stebbins."

"I figure they'd make tough chewing."

Wobbly Head said, "I've seen pictures of cannibals cookin' missionaries, clothes an' all in a cookin' kettle. Why don't you do the same to Brennan an' Stebbins?"

"We haven't got a big enough kettle. Listen, Kimlock all joking aside, you're putting Stirrup City's good townspeople in a bad spot. Gardens are eaten, all beef is gone, yesterday we butchered our last horse, now we're looking at the poor dogs."

"Blame it on your saloon-keeper an' banker," Luke Kimlock said.

"Can't we get word out to the sheriff?"

Kimlock grinned. "Sheriff got word of this blockade days an' days ago. He won't come out. I slugged him once, down in Beaverton. I tol' him then if he ever got in my way I'd kill him."

"He could send out a posse to drive you and Quarter Circle V out of here, couldn't he?"

Wobbly Head laughed. "I doubt if anybody in Beaverton except his cronies in that crooked court house would even lissen to him, doc. He stole the election, they say in Beaverton—because his side counted the votes."

Doctor Miller nodded thoughtfully. "Then it's no dice?"

"No dice," Luke Kimlock assured.

16

THE ninth night of the blockade Deacon Stebbins slowly lowered his violin, hearing hard boots hammer upward on the back staircase. Yellow lamplight showed hard glints shining angrily in his dark, brooding eyes.

He recognized the footsteps of the guard. The others belonged to none other than Silver Brennan who apparently was so angry he tried to drive his bootheels through the stair risers.

Deacon Stebbins leaned forward, carefully put his violin on the stand, then picked up his double-barreled shotgun, leaning against his chair. He put the loaded twelve-gauge across his skinny thighs, barrel pointing toward the door.

He was sure the first thing Silver Brennan would see, upon entering, was the scattergun's deadly bore. And in this assumption he did not err.

"Come in, Silver."

Silver Brennan fairly broke into the room.

217

He stopped abruptly, bootheels anchored in northern Montana's only carpeted floor, and said, "Deacon, you got to quit playin' that damn violin, man!"

"Why?" Deacon Stebbins gestured to the guard. The guard closed the door and returned downstairs to his post.

"Why? Because you're drivin' the townspeople crazy, that's why. Each time you play they think of you an' me an' the terrible predicament we got them into. Some are damn near starvin to death!"

"Are you?"

"Naturally not. You got quite a cache of grub up here. But for God's sake, don't let them know—or they'll storm the place with rifles an' shotguns an' pistols an' clubs."

"We got only about two days grub left."

Silver Brennan's eyes narrowed. "That all, Deacon? You ain't lyin' to me? You on the up-an'-up?"

"I'm stating the truth, Silver. You smuggled out too much for that favorite female of yours upstairs in your saloon. Two days, if we're not eating too much."

"Then what?"

Deacon Stebbins smiled faintly. "We starve

to death with the others, I guess. Or make a run of their blockade. Did you send out another man to contact the sheriff, like I said?"

"I did. Sent out Carter. An' you know what the sonofagun did? He joined up with Kimlock."

"How'd you know?"

"I was on my saloon's roof. With my field glasses. An' off in the distance—beyon' rifle range—who rides the circle but Carter."

Deacon Stebbins' gnarled fingers caressed his shotgun's smooth barrel and polished stock. "Well, we know where he is and what he's doing, which is more than we can say about your swamper and bartender we sent out three days ago. You seen hide or hair of them?"

"Seen them both, from my roof."

"That right?"

"They were both tied belly down over their saddles. Kimlock led one of their broncs, thet halfwit the other. An' both never moved, Deacon."

"Dead, you figure?"

"Stone dead, Deacon."

Deacon Stebbins' fingers moved. "How's the townspeople holding out? Any complaints?"

"Complaints?" Silver Brennan laughed

cynically. "Have I heard anything but complaints? You're up here alone—isolated—I'm down there where the action is, gettin' the works."

"Any talk of rebellion?"

"Not aroun' me there ain't. I'd gun dead the first bastard who bellyached, an' they know it. But I got spies out. They tell me all the things."

"Such as what?"

"The only beef in town walks daily back an' forth to the town pasture, like Kimlock lets them. All other's been eat."

"Butcher the milk cows."

Silver Brennan walked to the window. He looked down on Stirrup City. The town had no lights. All kerosene had been burned. There was no fat to make candles. The fat had all been consumed.

He turned, faced the banker. "You talk nutty as a loon, Deacon. We kill one of them milk cows, an' the people will rise up in arms, as the sayin' goes. Maybe you don't know it, but some people put their kids ahead of themselves, mister."

"Eat the horses."

"They ain't but two horses in town an' they're behin' in your stable under the rifle of your guard. All others have been eat. I don't know if it's true or not but the Higgins family is said to have cooked the family dog yesterday —that big, shaggy hair mutt that always lifts his leg against a post on my saloon, the bastard."

"There are more dogs, aren't there?"

"Nobody claims to be eatin' dog but I notice the canine population has sure fallen in number the last few days."

"Injuns eat dog. What's good enough for them is too good for the scum in this burg."

"You kinda forget one thing, Deacon."

"What's that?"

"This scum—as you call it—made you a rich man payin' interest on that money we came here with an' it was ill-got money, as they say."

Deacon Stebbins glanced hurriedly toward the door. "For hell's sake, Silver, watch your mouth! Somebody might be listening!"

Silver Brennan grinned. "Casper's back down in the alley. I heard him go down. An' the night air hasn't got ears, Deacon."

"Kimlock was in Beaverton. He could have sent out tracers on us on the railroad wire there. He's bound to have friends in the lawman ranks, him being a ranger, like he is."

"He sent them out, Deacon. The operator

sent a cowboy out to tell me. Kimlock held a gun over him"

Deacon Stebbins' fingers momentarily trembled, the dim lamplight hiding their shaking from Silver Brennan's eyes. "Wonder if any word has come back through the wire to Kimlock?"

"I don't know. Nobody can get in to tell us."

Deacon Brennan got shakily to his boots, shotgun cradled under his right armpit as a crutch, barrel down. "We got to kill Kimlock, Silver. We figured to trap him at Circle Diamond but the boys and you hit too fast. You should have waited until he'd come back from Beaverton."

"Lots of things we should have done an' didn't do," Silver Brennan said. "But what're we goin' do now?"

"What do you think, partner?"

"A spy tells me the townspeople are goin' have a meetin' tomorrow night in the church. They're talkin' about jus' walkin' out, hands high, with white rags, an' givin' up to Kimlock."

"Then what?"

"They might jus' sit aroun' an' wait an' live off the land, like Kimlock an' his riders do. Or

222

they might join forces with Kimlock in smokin' out you an' me so they can get back to their houses, Deacon."

Deacon Stebbins nodded. "Who's going to head the meeting?"

"Doc Miller."

"We could kill him. An example to anybody turning against us, you know. Put the fear of death in them."

"Deacon, talk sense."

"What's wrong with that plan?"

"Look, Deacon, look. You lost your head once. You shot Tim O'Rourke out of the saddle right in broad daylight on Main Street. Some still talk about you murderin' him. They didn't like it."

"What they like and what they get are two different things. All right, you're so damned smart, what do you say?"

"We can't whip the whole world. So if you can't whip 'em, let's join 'em. I'll attend the meetin'."

"They might string you up, Brennan."

"I'll take that chance. I'll report back later."

Silver Brennan returned to his saloon. His madame met him at the door. "The girls. They ain't got no grub, Mr. Brennan. '

223

"Neither have I" Silver Brennan was abrupt. "An' what is more, there seems little chance of any gettin' through."

"What'll I tell 'em?"

"Damn if I'd know, Minnie. Jes' make up some lies about grub comin', or some such thing."

"I've done that too often. None believes me, boss."

Silver Brennan spent the rest of the night playing poker in his saloon. The stakes were small. Very few in Stirrup City had any money. The reason was simple: his saloon had cleaned most pockets through its crooked games and shady dealers.

His upstairs safe contained most of Stirrup City's money. And the irony of the thing was that the money at present had little, if any, value. You can't buy turnips when there are no turnips for sale, he reasoned sourly.

His madame came downstairs at seven. "The girls ain't got a thing but cockroaches to eat," she complained. "I mean it—not a bit of bread, no flour, a little coffee, nothin' more."

Silver Brennan leaned back in his chair, eyes closed—a plan developing. Finally he opened his eyes.

"Get all the girls to pack what little they got. Get them to wear less clothes than the law allows. Then point them toward Signal Hump on foot an' I got a hunch Kimlock's men'll feed them."

"You issued an order that nobody could leave town. If they even tried, they'd be shot down."

"I take back that order, as of now but only where it deals with you an' your girls."

The madame's small eyes showed interest. "Them boys out there ain't had a woman for a long, long time, I'd say. I thank you, Silver."

The heavy set madame hurriedly returned upstairs. Silver Brennan went upstairs to Deacon Stebbins' quarters, where the Deacon was eating from an oval can of sardines.

"The last, Silver."

Brennan told the banker what he'd done. They watched the prostitutes leave town through the apartment's west window, Deacon Stebbins' eyes narrowed with thought.

"Ain't they some place in history where one army turned a whole passel of women loose on their enemy army an' the enemy went wild an' while the soldiers was with the women the other army come in an' kilt them all?" Silver Brennan wanted to know.

"I don't remember," Deacon Stebbins said, smiling wryly. "Time was when I had nothin' to do but read, remember?"

"Or to make little rocks outa big ones," Silver Brennan said, grinning. "There they go t'ward Signal Hump."

Signal Hump was a slanting hill west of Stirrup City. Children bobsledded and skied down it during snow season. Summer times they had bonfires on it and popped popcorn and had picnics.

Signal Hump was well beyond rifle shot. Silver Brennan knew from experience. Quarter Circle V men had a camp on the hill's crest. Silver Brennan had even seen his rifle balls plow up dirt at the hill's base, falling short of their mark.

The girls made a colorful, almost naked, group as they trudged out of Stirrup City, each carrying either a bundle or a small grip.

"Prostitutes never have much of a wardrobe," Deacon Stebbins mused.

Silver Brennan grinned. "The less, the better."

The banker permitted a small smile. The girls, about twenty in number, now neared the base of Signal Hump, but no Quarter Circle V

226

men came down to meet them, a fact which changed Silver Brennan's grin to a deep frown.

"Maybe all Kimlock hands are out on circle," Deacon Stebbins said.

The girls had halted at the hill's base. They stood on the road running to Hangton. The madame cupped her big hands to her big mouth. "Where you girl-hungry men at?"

Brennan and Stebbins now watched through powerful field glasses that brought the scene in very clearly.

The voice of a hidden man came from the thick brush on the hill's crest. "Come on up, females."

The words came clearly through the thin morning air. Silver Brennan said, "Sounded like Kimlock's voice?"

"The girls are goin' up," the banker said.

The girls climbed slowly, giggling and pushing, and finally disappeared into the brush. Silver Brennan lowered his glasses, grinning. "Soon the others out on circle will ride in, Deacon. Then the orgy will begin. I fergot to tell you the madame carried three gallons of Old Horseshoe in her sack."

"Hope it works so we can sneak out while they're drunk."

"It's gotta work, Deacon!"

They watched for an hour. They saw no more of the women. "Brush so high it hides 'em," Silver Brennan said.

Quarter Circle V guards rode into the brush. But strangely, they rode out again in a short while—a very short while—to continue riding circle beyond rifle range.

"I don't understand it," Silver Brennan said. "Look at that fink, Deacon? He rode in not more'n three minutes ago, now he's ridin' out ag'in. A man can't do nothin' in such a short time."

Deacon Stebbins wet his lips. "You're right, Silver. Look yonder toward the east I'll be damned if the females ain't there along the road! An' here comes the Hangton bound stage, sure as shootin'!"

Silver Brennan swung his glasses east. The stage came to a halt, the women climbing in, the big madame the last with her sack, which looked as full as when she'd left.

"She ain't left a drop of booze on the hill," Brennan said shortly. "That's Kimlock himself herdin' the girls onto that stage!"

"Him an' that halfwit Wobbly Head," the banker said.

The last girl aboard, the madame riding up on the box with the driver, the stage rocked out, heaving toward Hangton, dust rising behind the Concord's spinning wheels and pounding hoofs. Soon it was but a trace of Montana dust hanging in Montana's cloudless blue.

Deacon Stebbins shotgunned back to his chair. "Well, that failed, Brennan. What's next?"

"I dunno, Deacon. Things don't look good."

Things looked worse the next night when the town met in the frame church. Stirrup City residents were a hungry, anxious lot, especially those couples with children, and almost all married folks had plenty of these.

Mary Burnett was gate-keeper. Her job was to keep Brennan-Stebbins' saloon people from attending. Therefore she stopped big Silver Brennan at the door.

"Sorry, Mr. Brennan, but you cannot enter." Mary explained why not.

"I'm trapped in this town, too. Many blame it on me an' Deacon Stebbins. Mr. Stebbins can't attend, and the reason is apparent, therefore I want to sit in, for I might have some plan you people'd be interested in."

229

"Nothing you can say or do would interest any of us, I feel sure."

Doctor Henry Miller said, "The lady is right, Silver."

Others standing around waiting for the meeting to begin joined in on Mary's side. Brennan wisely withdrew. Doc Miller then called the meeting to order. All trooped inside, even young children. Silver Brennan had a wry thought: where the belly was concerned, all had interest . . . even young children.

The town was silent. All except those in his saloon were in church. He looked up at Deacon Stebbins' window.

He couldn't make out the crippled man, but he did see the drapes move a little.

He was all alone in front of the church. He knew better than try to force his way in. He realized suddenly and with sinking heart that no longer were he and Deacon Stebbins the bosses of Stirrup City.

Luke Kimlock's gun and hunger, had dethroned them.

Because of the heat, the front and back door of the church were open. He circled to the back door. He flattened against the wall beside the door jamb to listen.

230

The meeting was getting loud and out of control. He heard somebody say, "Let's watch our words, people. Silver Brennan was out in front, remember—and what we say we surely don't want him to hear."

Silver Brennan heard Doc Miller say, "One man go to the front and look out, and I'll look out the back."

When the doctor looked out, Silver Brennan was hidden in the shed behind the church, watching through a crack. Doc Miller pulled in his head. Brennan returned to his post beside the door, now closed.

Various plans were broached by various citizens. Finally Doc Miller advanced his plan, and Silver Brennan listened carefully.

The doctor pointed out that under threat of death he could not treat patients except those Brennan and Stebbins favored. "I'm false to my medical oath, but I have a family and my family needs me just as your family needs you, gentlemen."

"Aye, aye!"

Brennan's jaw stiffened. Doc Miller began pointing out pertinent facts, all black marks against a certain saloon-keeper and banker. Carefully, the doctor summer up a case not against Luke Kimlock but against the Silver Brennan–Deacon Stebbins conclave.

Angor tore at Silver Brennan. He made a vow to kill the doctor the first chance he got. From ambush, of course. Then, his blood chilled for a stern masculine voice said, "We should lynch Brennan an' Stebbins!"

"Now, now, Mr. Henderson," Doc Miller said. Brennan heard Henderson say, "We talk about a blockade set up by Kimlock an' Quarter Circle V. Quarter Circle V don't want us townsfolk. Kimlock an' his riders want Silver Brennan an' Deacon Stebbins."

"Here, hear!"

"Circle Diamon' killed ol' Cy Blunt. We know that. We figger Circle Diamon'—Stebbins an' Brennan—murdered Mary's father for his small ranch. The truth of the situation is this, people, if Brennan an' Stebbins remain in town, the sore, the canker, will still be with us."

"He's right, chairman," a woman said.

Brennan heard Doc Miller ask, "What's your solution, Mr. Henderson?"

Henderson's words were abrupt. "Lynch Stebbins an' Brennan!"

"Henderson's right!"

"That's the answer, people!"

232

"An' string 'em up, right now!"

"Get a rope, somebody! Let's move, people!"

Silver Brennan had heard enough. He left on the dead run.

17

LATE in the afternoon of the blockade's ninth day Mary Burnett met tall Luke Kimlock in the brush along the creek, Montana sunshine blessing her wealth of dark hair.

Kimlock came into the brush leading his buckskin. "Nobody saw you leave?" he asked.

Mary laughed quietly. "If one of their guards had seen me, I wouldn't be here. Your blockade is working."

"Yeah?"

"Only one thing wrong, the townspeople are suffering." She told of the shortage of food.

Luke Kimlock nodded. "They can come out any time they want. We have plenty of meat and flour. Uncle Cy had a root cellar on Quarter Circle V. A rock room, dug into a hill. It's full of spuds and such from his garden. Send the people out."

Mary nodded, deliberately evading Luke Kimlock's gray eyes. They had met in secret

234

rendezvous four previous times to bring Kimlock up-to-date on Stirrup City under siege.

She had liked him upon first meeting him the day he'd knocked Silver Brennan through the glass door of her cafe. Now she was afraid her liking him was changing to something deeper. And she didn't know just what to think.

She wondered if Luke did not feel the same toward her. She wished she could think clearly and level headedly about Luke Kimlock, but she couldn't. She kept remembering a saying of her murdered father.

Curt Burnett had said that when a man was in love he needed all his senses but because of love he had control of none of them. Now Mary wondered if this didn't hold true for women, as well.

"What else?" Luke Kimlock asked.

She told him of the proposed town meeting in the church that night. "And some talk of lynching Brennan and Stebbins, Luke."

Luke Kimlock looked across into space and then thoughtfully said, "I can understand why. Who's behin' such talk?"

"Mr. Henderson. I hardly believe you've met him."

"I haven't I wish they wouldn't do it, though."

"Why?"

"Well, for one thing, it's takin' the law in private hands, Mary. An' that isn't good. The men lynchin' them would bear the scar of the event all their lives. Their children would say, 'There goes one of the men who lynched Brennan an' Stebbins.'"

Mary's face was very serious. "I understand. But you hope to kill them, so I fail to see the difference."

"All the difference in the world. Brennan and Stebbins lifted guns against me an' Quarter Circle V. They murdered my uncle. An eye for an eye and a tooth for a tooth still holds in my case."

"But you're a man of the law, a ranger?"

"A man, first—a ranger, second."

Mary's lips pursed. "It's too much for me, Luke. I guess a woman can never, never understand a man's viewpoint. But if you killed Brennan—or Stebbins—or both, wouldn't your conscience also bear the scar you mentioned?"

"No."

"Why, may I ask?"

"I'd give them a fair fight. A rope is the sneaky way—a lynch-rope, that is."

"I understand that. This is coming to a head, Luke." Now she looked up at him. "Each time I leave you I wonder if I'll ever see you alive again."

"Would it matter, Mary?"

"Yes, it would—much, to me."

There, the words were out! At last, she'd said what she'd wanted. She was aware of her cheeks becoming red. And what was the matter with Luke Kimlock? He just stood there, the tall, handsome sap!

A terrible thought hit her. She realized she knew very little about Luke Kimlock's past. Was he married? Had he a wife? Good heavens, had she fallen in love for nothing?

Then, Luke moved.

She had to stand on tiptoe to meet his lips. Then, she stepped back, saying, "I'm sorry, Luke."

"For what?"

She laughed quietly. "For leading you on, you big oaf!" Then, without another word, she wheeled, skirt swinging, and ran out of sight into the high concealing buckbrush.

She left behind a grinning, happy Luke

Kimlock. Mary had just beat him to the confession, he realized. He'd held back for one simple reason: he might not have long to live.

A bullet has no conscience, he well knew. A bullet killed whoever it hit, be that person male or female, rich or poor, stupid or educated. And what woman wants to be a widow even before being married?

Luke's grin widened. Such a thing was impossible, he told himself—he was mixing up similies and metaphors, nothing more. He whirled, hand going to his holster, as he heard brush crackle behind him.

He at first thought Mary had returned but then he heard Wobbly Head call out, "Brother Luke?"

"Here, boy."

Wobbly Head parted buckbrush. "Done caught me a prisoner back along the crick. Mind who he was, brother?"

Luke said stiffly, "This is a serious thing, boy—so let's play no guessin' games, please."

"I caught Barnhart."

Luke smiled. Joe Barnhart was one of Brennan's top guns. "No bullets fired, brother?"

"I snuck up behin' him. Almost bent my

gun-barrel as I slammed him over his thick skull."

"Where's he now?"

"Barefooted, an' hikin' through the prickly-pear cactus toward Hangton, minus his gun an' his pants and with a big headache."

"Good deal, brother Elmer."

"How come you gave me orders not to kill anybody but Brennan or Stebbins, brother Luke?"

"I don't want a cold-blooded death on your conscience all the rest of your life. It's one thing to kill in protection of your life or to avenge the murder of a friend, but cold-blooded killing is a horse of another color, an' I'm not repeatin' that again savvy?"

"Ah, brother Luke, hol' your hosses. Say, them wild women, goin' on that stage this mornin'—Some of the boy's kinda mad yet with you for not keepin' them females."

"Let them get sore."

"An' some wanted that booze."

Luke's grin widened. "Don't tell them, but I cached the booze beyon' a hill back of Signal Hump. When this is over, the boys can get drunk to their toenails."

"You don't say." Wobbly Head's eyes

widened. "What'd the madame have in her sack when she climbed up on the stage?"

"A few rocks to make it look as though the sack was still heavy. An' some doubled up brush to give the sack a full look."

"I'll be hanged."

"You keep that secret, understand? I don't want our men searchin' for a booze cache and not ridin' gun circle."

"I won't talk, brother. What'd you doin' alone here in this bresh?"

"For me to know. For you to guess."

Wobbly Head pouted. "That ain't a nice answer, brother Luke. Me, I aim to kill Silver Brennan."

"I thought Deacon Stebbins was your meat? That's what you said this mornin', remember?"

"I wanna kill them both."

"Get out on patrol."

Wobbly Head bowed deeply. "As you say, my Lord." Grinning, he walked into the brush and out of sight.

Luke Kimlock yawned. He was bearded, dirty and tired. The nine days had been long and sleepless. What sleep he'd got had been in scattered and short winks.

His men were getting weary of this, he knew.

If this were not settled within a few days he feared some Quarter Circle V cowboys would ride out and leave him alone with Wobbly Head.

Almost a week and a half had passed since Circle Diamond's raid had killed Uncle Cy, their boss and the effect created in the cowboys by Uncle Cy's tragic death was beginning to wear thin, Luke reckoned.

He swung up on his buckskin. Within the hour he'd roped a Brennan card dealer hoping to sneak out of Stirrup City. The man was on foot. He'd seen Kimlock riding through the brush along the creek.

He'd started to run. Kimlock had galloped down on him, lass-rope swinging. The man had seen then that escape was impossible. He'd stopped. He'd put his hands high and screamed, "I don't pack a gun, Mr. Kimlock!"

Kimlock's noose shot out. The man jumped as the loop came in around his feet. Kimlock had wanted him to jump because then the noose snaked under the man's shoes.

Thus Luke Kimlock roped the man around the ankles. His front footing horses in corrals had come in handy. He jerked in slack. The man went down, both ankles pinned.

"Mr. Kimlock, don't kill me, please! I'll tell you anythin' I know, sir."

Kimlock dismounted. The man tried to stand. Kimlock jerked on the rope. The gambler went down again. This time the gambler landed hard on his wide behind.

Kimlock pulled his .45. He had no intention to shoot the man in cold blood; he merely wanted to put the fear of death into him. Nevertheless, he deliberately shot.

Dirt spouted around the man's feet. He screamed, "For Lord's sake, don't kill me," and then he said, "Kimlock, you shot the heel off one of my shoes!"

Grinning, Kimlock punched the spent cartridge out, inserted a new one, closed his gun's loading gate. "How are Brennan an' Stebbins?"

"I don't know. I jus' deal cards. The town is starvin', Kimlock. I guess Stebbins an' Brennan ain't got too much to chew on, either. Or why'd they chase out the girls?"

"Any horses left in town?"

"Only two, they tell me."

"Who owns them?"

"Stebbins. An' Brennan. They're under

guard in Stebbins' stable, rifle guard. All the rest have been et."

"Where were you going?"

"Tryin' to sneak out, of course. Anythin' is better'n eatin' card chips." The gambler grinned. "You could cook a chip all day an' it'd not soften up, eh?"

Twilight was changing to darkness. Luke pumped the man for facts. He repeated what Mary Burnett had told him.

Stirrup City residents were in bad shape.

"Take off your shoes an' pants," Luke said.

The gambler stared at him. "Why?"

"You're goin' back into Stirrup City."

"Barefooted? An' with no pants on? I'll be the laughin' stock of the town, Kimlock!"

"Which would you rather be, laughed at or dead?"

The gambler studied Luke Kimlock's rough face. "By hell, you'd kill me, Kimlock."

He took off his shoes and dropped his pants. Luke rode behind him toward Stirrup City, the man picking his way across cactus beds. Each time he slowed down, Luke Kimlock's catch-rope snapped across the bare rump.

"Why you doin' this to me, Kimlock?"

"You're settin' an example, gambler. You're

showin' the rest of the Stebbins–Brennan pack
of thieves there's no use tryin' to escape."

"I never did have no luck," the gambler
mourned.

"Get movin'."

18

SILVER BRENNAN kept himself in superb physical shape. He sprinted the distance from the church to Deacon Stebbin's bank in record time, pausing only once when a man's voice called from between the Mercantile and the hardware store, "Hey, Silver, help me."

Silver Brennan stopped. One of his gamblers —a fat one—stood between the two buildings. He had no socks, shoes, pants or underwear.

"What the hell—?"

"Luke Kimlock. I went to the crick hopin' to catch a fish. He roped me an' undressed me an' . . . Hey, Silver, don't run off! Help me, man!"

But Silver Brennan was gone. Deacon Stebbins' guard sat dozing, back to the alley barn. Brennan jerked him awake. "Harness the team, quick. An' damn quick, too. To the buggy—the high-wheeled one. Get to work."

"What's the hurry?"

"Get movin', or I'll kill you."

"No need to do that," the guard said, darting into the barn. Silver Brennan ran up the stairs.

Deacon Stebbins heard the harsh words down in the alley and was at the door when the saloon owner burst in. Panting the words, Brennan told the banker about the lynching plans.

"We gotta get out, Deacon!"

Deacon Stebbins merely nodded. "Been expectin' this for some time, Silver. We should have a little time, yet." He looked at his violin. "You're comin' with me."

"Don't drag that damn' fiddle along. We gotta make tracks, Deacon." Silver Brennan went to the fireman's pole in the middle of the room. He slid down it into the bank below.

Upstairs, Deacon Stebbins looked at his violin, then at his shotgun, and he said, "Violin, you stay behin'."

He picked up the double-barreled shotgun. He slid down the fireman's pole. Already Silver Brennan was at the safe. "You know the combination, Deacon. I don't."

Within seconds, the safe door swung open. Brennan scooped out a small bag of gold eagles, Deacon Stebbins taking the forged will. "Might need this," the banker said.

"Need dinero most," Silver Brennan said.

They'd already made their plans of escape. They'd talked them over from end to end up in Deacon's quarters. They'd left nothing to chance. They had known they might win and they'd known they might suffer defeat. Only a fool didn't plan, both had long ago learned.

They went out the bank's back door, the banker locking it behind them. The team of black geldings stood in the alley hitched to a light buggy.

"Pullin' out?" the guard asked.

"None of your damn business," Silver Brennan snapped. "Here, help me get Deacon into the buggy! Make yourself useful!"

"Not on the seat," the banker said. "Let me lay down on my belly. I might have to do some shootin'! Hard for me to shoot sittin' down."

"Okay, Deacon," Brennan said.

Brennan grabbed the reins. "Get a-movin', you black boneheaded bastards!" His buggy whip cracked.

The blacks leaped against collars. Tugs tightened. Wheels spun. Silver Brennan braced his boots hard against the dashboard. A Winchester .30–30 rode beside him on the leather-covered seat. Two guns hung from his blocky hips, the two cylinders filled with .45 cartridges.

Their plan called that they take the Beaverton road out of town. They had but to cross a tree free strip of about a hundred yards and then they'd be deep in the cottonwoods and box-elders along Stirrup River.

To leave, they had to pass the church. Citizens were just beginning to leave the building when the buggy wheeled past, iron rims kicking up dirt and gravel, the blacks running with ears laid back and tails extended.

"Hey, look at that buggy!"

"Jim, that's Deacon Stebbins' rig. An' that's that bastardly Brennan on the lines. But where's the Deacon?"

A six-gun roared. Brennan never did know where its bullet went, and didn't care for neither he nor his passenger or a horse was hit. He stood now, whip pounding the black rumps.

Brennan's plan was simple. Once free of town he'd murder Deacon Stebbins. The gold would be all his. He'd have the will, too. He'd leave the rig and the dead man in the timber.

He'd sneak on foot through the high brush to the river. He'd swim Stirrup River and get into the badlands on the north shore. There he'd hide successfully, he knew. He'd work his way to Beaverton.

Back in Stirrup City, Deacon Stebbins' safe held a small fortune. Nobody in town knew the combination. Unless they used dynamite, they'd never open the safe.

The small fortune therein would hire guns and gunmen in Beaverton. Again, the sheriff and county officials would be paid and paid well to look the other way.

The main thing was to run this blockade, cross the grassy strip, get into Stirrup River's thick brush.

And get back to that safe, too.

For he knew the safe's combination. Around Deacon Stebbins he'd said he had had no idea how to open the safe but he'd covertly watched the banker turn the dial and he'd learned the combination.

He looked down at Deacon Stebbins. The banker lay on his belly, shotgun angled over the wooden panel of the buggy. Temptation tugged him. He could easily put a .45 bullet through the back of the banker's head.

He swallowed, desire strong. Common sense then came in. Guns might talk while they ran

Luke Kimlock's blockade. And two guns were better and more deadly than one.

He'd kill Deacon Stebbins in the river brush. They'd find his dead body and think that Luke Kimlock or a Quarter Circle V gunman had killed the banker. He whipped for more speed.

No more shots came from the church. One block of buildings lay between the church and the edge of town, and that edge was rapidly approaching.

Silver Brennan, standing wide-legged in the pitching rig, glanced up, noting the moon. It still had not gained brilliance. Now the hundred yards of grassy area came roaring up to meet the plunging horses, and the saloon man's heart suddenly took a lurch.

For two riders had miraculously appeared out of the eastern buckbrush. He immediately recognized them despite the dim moonlight. One rode a blue roan; the other a cream-colored buckskin.

For Luke Kimlock and Wobbly Head had heard the shot from the crowd in front of the church. They'd been riding circle together. Luke had reined in his buckskin and asked, "Wonder why they're shootin' at, brother Elmer?"

250

"Do I hear a rig comin' this direction?"

"You sure do, brother Elmer, an' here it comes now!"

Wobbly Head stood on his oxbow stirrups. "Right you are, brother Luke. Hey, ain't that Deacon Stebbins' buggy?"

"I don't know. You know the horses an' rigs aroun' here, I don't. But one thing is, regardless of who it is, he ain't runnin' our blockade. Come on!"

They spurred forward, heading northwest, the buggy and running horses about an eighth of a mile ahead, speeding across the sagebrush area for the tall timber along the river.

"That's Deacon's rig!" Wobbly Head hollered. "An' if my eyes are right, that's Brennan standin' drivin'!"

"He get in thet bresh," Luke Kimlock hollered, "an' he might get away, boy."

Suddenly, Wobbly Head's horse stumbled, then fell tail over tincup, throwing the youth wide, Wobbly Head sliding in the brush on his belly and Luke Kimlock's buckskin plunged on alone, reins around the saddle-horn, Luke's six-shooter spouting flame.

Luke figured Brennan's gun had knocked down Wobbly Head's roan, for Brennan was shooting. Brennan had dropped the reins and evidently had put his boot on them so they'd not bounce from the fast-moving rig.

Thus, he had both hands free and both hands then clutched a roaring, spitting, fire-dealing six-shooter.

Luke knew he was taking his life in his hands, but if Brennan once escaped it might be impossible to corral him again. He had to take a chance. Suddenly, he felt his buckskin lurch.

His terrifying thought was that the buckskin had been hit. Then he realized his saddle-fork was shattered. Brennan's bullet had torn into the front of his saddle.

Fear tore at him. Two inches higher, and the bullet would have ripped his guts in two.

He didn't look back at Wobbly Head. He didn't have time. He'd counted his bullets. He had two left.

Slowly, he gained on the plunging buggy. Rising on stirrups, he tried to take aim, his buckskin now on his regular even stride.

He let his hammer fall.

Suddenly, Silver Brennan staggered. Then, the saloon man screamed—a high-pitched sound cutting across space.

Brennan dropped his smoking six-shooters.

Then, he pitched sidewise as the buggy wheels hit a rut.

The lurching rig threw the saloon man sidewise. Then, as the rig righted, it pitched him off its side. Brennan hit the ground, face down.

The horses ran wildly on, heading for Stirrup River's timber, the rig bouncing and leaping, the team without a driver.

Luke Kimlock had figured Brennan alone in the rig. Then, he heard a voice scream, "Brennan, where are you?"

Luke realized the yell had come from the buggy's bed. Now a shotgun was pointed at him over the buggy's low box.

The double-barreled shotgun belched roaring flame his direction, but if the buckshot came close Luke did not hear it for his horse's hoofs pounding the dry soil made too much racket.

He realized Deacon Stebbins lay hidden in the buggy box, and the buggy would soon reach timber. He had long figured that the banker was not as crippled as he professed. He had a hunch that once Deacon Stebbins got in the timber he'd be awful hard to find, if indeed he could be found.

Despair hit Luke Kimlock. The buggy was escaping. Then, a strange thing happened. For a man ran out of the brush toward the buggy. Luke recognized Wobbly Head.

Luke Kimlock pulled his buckskin back on his haunches, his smoking six-gun upraised, one bullet left in its cylinder. He dared not shoot now. He might hit Wobbly Head.

He glanced back. Wobbly Head's roan stood with his nigh foreleg raised. Luke then realized Wobbly Head had made the distance on the run, cutting across at an angle.

He also noticed the youth carried no weapon. Evidently the youth had lost his six-gun when his bronc had fallen. And he'd not had time to pull his rifle from his saddle boot.

The fast moving rig was twenty feet or so from the brush when the boy jumped on the double tree, just in front of the buggy's dashboard. Despite the pressure against the clevis pin, he managed to pull it free, loosening the double tree—and the team plunged ahead minus the buggy, hooked together by the neck yoke which had slid from the tongue's end.

The tongue instantly hit the dirt. For one moment, the buggy was suspended in air standing on its tongue. Then, the tongue broke with a loud snap, but not before a screaming Deacon Stebbins had been thrown free.

Wobbly Head also went down with the buggy, the rig shattering into bits over him and the banker. Luke Kimlock spurred forward, heart in his throat, for both banker and youth lay prone, not moving.

He left saddle on the dead run, his trailing reins setting the buckskin on sliding haunches. Behind him came townspeople running and shouting. Silver Brennan had not moved.

Wobbly Head lay on his belly. Deacon Stebbins was a broken, unmoving piece of humanity, his black suit heavy with blood. Gently, Luke Kimlock turned the youth, who stared up at him in the moonlight.

"Brother Luke?"

"Yes, brother Elmer?"

BROTHER . . . Luke really meant the word, now. His throat was dry. Fear clutched him. The youth looked badly hurt.

"My roan—He stumbled over a greasewood an' went down—They were gittin' away—I ran like hell, brother Luke—"

"I saw you. Be quiet now, boy."

"I'm not beat up too bad. I saw Brennan fall. You made a good shot from that distance."

"Lots of luck, brother Elmer."

"But Deacon—?"

255

"Hey's layin' behin' you, boy."

Wobbly Head twisted his head around to look. Doctor Henry Miller knelt beside the inert Deacon Stebbins. Other townspeople had arrived. They stood panting and watching the doctor.

Finally Doc Miller got to his feet. He slowly shook his head and then moved over and knelt beside Wobbly Head. "Boy, you sure were up in the air," he said. "Here, don't move, please."

"I flew high," Wobbly Head said.

A man said, "We owe you an' Mr. Kimlock a great debt, boy. I don't know how we can ever pay you."

Luke Kimlock said nothing. Wobbly Head lay with his eyes closed. Doctor Miller looked at the boy's ears and said, "No blood. No concussion. That left arm looks odd, twisted like that. I'd say it was broken."

Wobbly Head spoke without opening his eyes. "Brennan, doc?"

"He'll deal no more cards," Doc Miller said. "Not here on this planet, anyway."

Wobbly Head opened his eyes. "You all done inspectin' my carcass, doc?" He looked at Mary

Burnett who knelt beside Luke Kimlock. "Look, doc, they're holdin' hands!"

Doc Miller smiled. "What's wrong with that?"

"Not a thing," Wobbly Head said. "I think it looks danged good!"

"So do I," the doctor said, "So do I."

THE END

Other titles in the
Linford Western Library:

TOP HAND
by Wade Everett

The Broken T was big enough for a man on
the run to hire out as a cowhand and be safe.
But no ranch is big enough to let a man hide
from himself.

GUN WOLVES OF LOBO BASIN
by Lee Floren

The Feud was a blood debt. When Smoke
Talbot found the outlaws who gunned down
his folks he aimed to nail their hide to the barn
door.

SHOTGUN SHARKEY
by Marshall Grover

The westbound coach carrying the indomit-
able Larry and Stretch and their mixed bag of
allies headed for a shooting showdown.

FIGHTING RAMROD
by Charles N. Heckelmann

Most men would have cut their losses, but Frazer counted the bullets in his guns and said he'd soak the range in blood before he'd give up another inch of what was his.

LONE GUN
by Eric Allen

Smoke Blackbird had been away too long. The Lequires had seized the Blackbird farm, forcing the Indians and settlers off, and no one seemed willing to fight! He had to fight alone.

THE THIRD RIDER
by Barry Cord

Mel Rawlins wasn't going to let anything stand in his way. His father was murdered, his two brothers gone. Now Mel rode for vengeance.

RIDE A LONE TRAIL
by Gordon D. Shirreffs

The valley was about to explode into open range war. All it needed was the fuse and Ken Macklin was it.

ARIZONA DRIFTERS
by W. C. Tuttle

When drifting Dutton and Lonnie Steelman decide to become partners they find that they have a common enemy in the formidable Thurston brothers.

TOMBSTONE
by Matt Braun

Wells Fargo paid Luke Starbuck to outgun the silver-thieving stagecoach gang at Tombstone. Before long Luke can see the only thing bearing fruit in this eldorado will be the gallows tree.

HIGH BORDER RIDERS
by Lee Floren

Buckshot McKee and Tortilla Joe cut the trail of a border tough who was running Mexican beef into Texas. They stopped the smuggler in his tracks.

HARD MAN WITH A GUN
by Charles N. Heckelmann

After Bob Keegan lost the girl he loved and the ranch he had sweated blood to build, he had nothing left but his guts and his guns but he figured that was enough.

BRETT RANDALL, GAMBLER
by E. B. Mann

Larry Day had the choice of running away from the law or of assuming a dead man's place. No matter what he decided he was bound to end up dead.

THE GUNSHARP
by William R. Cox

The Eggerleys weren't very smart. They trained their sights on Will Carney and Arizona's biggest blood bath began.

THE DEPUTY OF SAN RIANO
by Lawrence A. Keating and
Al. P. Nelson

When a man fell dead from his horse, Ed Grant was spotted riding away from the scene. The deputy sheriff rode out after him and came up against everything from gunfire to dynamite.

SUNDANCE: IRON MEN
by Peter McCurtin

Sundance, assigned to save the railroad from a murder spree, soon came to realise that he'd have to fight fire with fire, bullets with bullets and death with death!

FARGO: MASSACRE RIVER
by John Benteen

Fargo spurred his horse to the edge of the road. The ambushers up ahead had now blocked the road. Fargo's convoy was a jumble, a perfect target for the insurgents' weapons!

SUNDANCE:
DEATH IN THE LAVA
by John Benteen

The land echoed with the thundering hoofs of Modoc ponies. In minutes they swooped down and captured the wagon train and its cargo of gold. But now the halfbreed they called Sundance was going after it, and he swore nothing would stand in his way.

GUNS OF FURY
by Ernest Haycox

Dane Starr, alias Dan Smith, wanted to close the door on his past and hang up his guns, but people wouldn't let him. Good men wanted him to settle their scores for them. Bad men thought they were faster and itched to prove it. Starr had to keep killing just to stay alive.

FARGO: PANAMA GOLD
by John Benteen

Cleve Buckner was recruiting an army of killers, gunmen and deserters from all over Central America. With foreign money behind him, Buckner was going to destroy the Panama Canal before it could be completed. Fargo's job was to stop Buckner—and to eliminate him once and for all!

FARGO: THE SHARPSHOOTERS
by John Benteen

The Canfield clan, thirty strong, were raising hell in Texas. One of them had shot a Texas Ranger, and the Rangers had to bring in the killer. Fargo was tough enough to hold his own against the whole clan.

SUNDANCE: OVERKILL
by John Benteen

Sundance's reputation as a fighting man had spread. There was no job too tough for the halfbreed to handle. So when a wealthy banker's daughter was kidnapped by the Cheyenne, he offered Sundance $10,000 to rescue the girl.

HELL RIDERS
by Steve Mensing

Wade Walker's kid brother, Duane, was locked up in the Silver City jail facing a rope at dawn. Wade was a ruthless outlaw, but he was smart, and he had vowed to have his brother out of jail before morning!

DESERT OF THE DAMNED
by Nelson Nye

The law was after him for the murder of a marshal—a murder he didn't commit. Breen was after him for revenge—and Breen wouldn't stop at anything . . . blackmail, a frameup . . . or murder.

DAY OF THE COMANCHEROS
by Steven C. Lawrence

Their very name struck terror into men's hearts—the Comancheros, a savage army of cutthroats who swept across Texas, leaving behind a bloodstained trail of robbery and murder.

SUNDANCE: SILENT ENEMY
by John Benteen

Both the Indians and the U.S. Cavalry were being victimized. A lone crazed Cheyenne was on a personal war path against both sides. They needed to pit one man against one crazed Indian. That man was Sundance.

LASSITER
by Jack Slade

Lassiter wasn't the kind of man to listen to reason. Cross him once and he'd hold a grudge for years to come—if he let you live that long. But he was no crueler than the men he had killed, and he had never killed a man who didn't need killing.

LAST STAGE TO GOMORRAH
by Barry Cord

Jeff Carter, tough ex-riverboat gambler, now had himself a horse ranch that kept him free from gunfights and card games. Until Sturvesant of Wells Fargo showed up. Jeff owed him a favour and Sturvesant wanted it paid up. All he had to do was to go to Gomorrah and recover a quarter of a million dollars stolen from a stagecoach!

McALLISTER ON THE COMANCHE CROSSING
by Matt Chisholm

The Comanche, deadly warriors and the finest horsemen in the world, reckon McAllister owes them a life—and the trail is soaked with the blood of the men who had tried to outrun them before.

QUICK-TRIGGER COUNTRY
by Clem Colt

Turkey Red hooked up with Curly Bill Graham's outlaw crew and soon made a name for himself. But wholesale murder was out of Turk's line, so when range war flared he bucked the whole border gang alone . . .

PISTOL LAW
by Paul Evan Lehman

Lance Jones came back to Mustang for just one thing—Revenge! Revenge on the people who had him thrown in jail; on the crooked marshal; on the human vulture who had already taken over the town. Now it was Lance's turn . . .